I0784208

The Butterfly Diary

Copyright © by Mari Nicolas

Cover design by Elizabeth Mackey

Editor Brianne Vander Neut

All rights reserved.
No part of this book may be reproduced in any form or
by any electronic or mechanical means including information
storage and retrieval systems, without permission in writing
from the author. The only exception is by a reviewer, who
may quote short excerpts in a review.

To Susan who always believed in me

To Chris who has my back every day

Contents

Prologue

In the dream, a Huna priestess stands before me. A leafy green haku crown made of ti leaves adorns her head. Her long ebony hair flows around her shoulders like a shawl. She is dressed in a long, white muumuu dress. We are standing in a dark, silent chamber. I suddenly realize we are in a mausoleum. She points down at my feet, and I realize that I'm standing over a sealed marble crypt. She leans close and whispers, "The secret is in the bones." I hear a noise and look up to see a crow sitting on the windowsill of an arched stone window above me. It begins to flap its wings loudly and ominously, then lifts up, flying away high in the sky. Its sleek black body dissolves into an orange butterfly and vanishes in a ray of brilliant sunlight.

Chapter One

"Babe, your sugar daddy is calling."

My eyes fluttered open, and my gaze fixed on Rodrigo, my much younger, handsome, thirty-eight year old lover, who was waving my cell phone at me with a grin.

"He's *not* my sugar daddy!" I retorted. "And he can call back."

My response made him laugh as he set my phone down on the nightstand next to the bed. Sometimes when I woke up, I'd look around at my room and wonder where I was. I still lived near my hometown of San Francisco but on the other side of the Golden Gate Bridge. It'd been only a year since I'd moved into the modest in-law unit, and I was still startled by the Ikea-furnished space, which reminded me of a spartan motel room. The bedframe, chest of drawers, and matching nightstands were all blocky, utilitarian pieces of light oak veneer. It also seemed surreal that I was divorced after twenty years and single again. My marriage had seemed divinely ordained and was even blessed by a Hindu priestess.

As I lay there, images from my dream I'd awoken from haunted me, and I wondered why I kept having the huna dream. What did it mean and why did it make me so uneasy?

"You were talking in your sleep again," Rodrigo said.

"I was?"

"Yeah. You kept saying, *'What… what… go away!'*"

I didn't answer.

"You had that weird dream again, huh?"

I wished I hadn't said anything to him. Being vulnerable with my feelings was an ongoing challenge since my divorce.

But as the aromatic smell of freshly brewed coffee permeated my apartment, I remembered that was what I loved about Rodrigo… he always brought food, and he always made a hearty breakfast the morning after our hookups.

It was a strange feeling when you were with a new lover. When Rodrigo and I had made love for the first time, it had been exciting and intense. I hadn't been with anyone except my husband of twenty years, and when I had undressed down to my bra and panties, he'd gently pushed me onto the bed and began kissing me so intensely I could hardly breathe. All I could think about was… did he mind that my stomach was round and soft? Did he think it was weird that I didn't shave *down there*? My worrisome thoughts had vanished as he sat up, lowered my panties, and put his face between my legs. I'd been so shocked, I'd tensed up with embarrassment. He'd pulled away and stared at me with concern.

"It's okay," I assured him. "I'm not used to this level of *enthusiasm.*"

"Better get used to it."

Then there was the awkward *morning after,* when you get up early, brush your teeth, comb your hair out, smooth on moisturizer, and slip back into bed.

That was months ago, and Rodrigo's presence in my tiny in-law apartment seemed natural now. I even left him a key under my coco coir doormat.

Now, he climbed back into bed with me and snuggled tightly against me, spoon-style.

"What's my girl want? I can make your blueberry pancakes and bacon. I can make you scrambled eggs and toast." He buried his nose in my hair. "I like your new shampoo."

My phone rang again, and I knew it was Markus.

"Man, he's persistent," Rodrigo said as he cupped my right breast in his hand gently. "He's missing *this*!" he teased.

I removed his hand. "What about those scrambled eggs?"

"You actually getting up?"

"Yes!"

He got up first, and I enjoyed the view of his toned physique moving toward the kitchen, wearing only a pair of pin-striped cotton shorts. He smelled freshly of my patchouli soap, and his thick black hair was slightly damp and tousled.

I sat up and reached for my cell phone. It looked like Markus had left me a voicemail. I could listen to it later, knowing he was out-of-town on business in Los Angeles.

I got up and went into the bathroom to brush my teeth and put on a bathrobe, then bent over and fluffed up my hair so that the waves fell loosely around my shoulders. My lash extensions were still intact, and I batted my eyes, laughing at my silly reflection in the mirror.

Rodrigo stood in the doorway with a mug of coffee.

"Hey, gorgeous. Almond milk—just like you like. It's a crime that you wake up looking so sexy like *that*."

He put the mug down on the edge of the bathroom sink, then stood over me and ran his fingers lightly through my tousled mop of hair.

"Hey, Kiki said thank you for mentioning her in your Yelp review. Our boss even brought it up at our last staff meeting."

"I was happy to do it—she deserves recognition. Isn't there some hospital rule about not fraternizing with patients?" I asked.

"You're not a patient anymore, and Kiki doesn't care. She thinks it's funny we hooked up."

My face flushed. "Because I'm so much older than you?"

He chuckled. "No, because she knew I kept eyeballing you when you were on the mat stretching. I told her you were one sexy mama!"

"You mean… a *MILF*."

We'd met at the county hospital physical therapy clinic, where he worked as a senior physical therapist and staff supervisor. He'd been sexy in pale-blue hospital scrubs, but it had been his warm smile and easy-going personality that attracted me. I had been getting treated for frozen shoulder— not by him but a talented and pretty young female physical therapist named Kiki. I'd thought for sure Rodrigo and Kiki were having a fling, having observed how playful they were toward each other, sharing private jokes or making silly faces.

It was weird how one day you were a sexy young thing and then the next day you were a MILF. Where had all the time gone? I was actually surprised that at fifty-five, I didn't feel old or decrepit. Perimenopause wasn't fun, and I'd gained thirty pounds, but not having menstrual cycles was great.

I smiled and thanked him as I took my coffee mug and went into the kitchen with Rodrigo trailing me.

"Man, you were sacked out last night after your bath!" Rodrigo said.

"I was? I don't remember."

"Really? I knocked on the bathroom door because I was worried. You were in the bathroom for almost an hour. When I peeked in, you were like… floating in the water with this funny, dreamy expression. You looked like a cute mermaid."

"It wasn't an hour… *was it*? More like thirty minutes."

He shrugged but smiled. I took a sip of fragrant coffee and savored the bittersweet French roast taste. Rodrigo was a genius at coffeemaking… among his other admirable traits.

"I've always loved being in the water. Kai and I learned to swim at the neighborhood recreation center. I picked it up quickly, much to my aunt's surprise. She actually got upset because I figured it out in one lesson. She'd paid for swim camp for the entire summer."

I recalled the first dip in the big lap pool and how buoyant and free I felt darting back and forth in the lap lanes. My swim instructor, a former competitive swimmer, even urged my aunt to enroll me in the swim club.

"My bestie used to call me *Minnow*. We used to go to swim camp every summer at the YMCA."

"I think you're more Ariel than a minnow," he said, referring to the *Little Mermaid* movie. He sat across from me, his hands cupped around the ceramic coffee mug. I noticed he was sipping from my sea turtle mug.

"She is… I wish we could spend more time together. But she got married and moved back to Hawaii. We were so close as kids," I said with a wistful sigh.

One of the unique features of my compact kitchen was a big, pop-up glass skylight over the stove. Rodrigo busied himself getting breakfast ingredients together while I sat at the pine, farmhouse-style kitchen table. A tapping noise got my attention, and I looked up at the skylight. There was a big black crow pecking at the skylight outside—like the one in my dream. I must have gasped because Rodrigo turned to look at me while he was cracking eggs into a ceramic mixing bowl.

"What?"

I pointed up at the skylight.

"I've seen him before. Hey, buddy!" He waved playfully at the crow, who ignored Rodrigo and continued to peck on the glass.

It seemed pretty insistent, so I walked over and waved up at him. "Hey there. You just saying hello or what? You got my attention."

The pecking stopped and the bird became still, staring down at me, his beady black eyes appraising.

"He likes you!" Rodrigo teased.

"Okay, let's agree to a truce. You quit pecking and let us eat our breakfast in peace. I'll leave you some birdseed outside."

"Actually, they like to eat peanuts, pecans, and berries, not birdseed," Rodrigo said.

"Okay, Mr. Crow… I'll leave some peanuts out if you go away *now*!"

As soon as I said that, he launched himself into the air and flew away. I went back to the dining table and saw my journal on one of the chairs, picking it up as Rodrigo popped two pieces of sourdough bread into the toaster oven.

"I was wiping down the table last night and moved your notebook. I meant to put it back. Sorry."

"It's my divorce journal. My therapist said I needed to process my angst by writing daily. I'm not sure how helpful it is, since all I do is vent about Jason and the divorce."

My therapist had gifted me the journal when I filed for divorce. It was a pretty, lined, spiral-bound notebook with butterflies on the cover and the words *"Spread your wings and fly!"* I flipped open the plastic cover and saw an old childhood picture of my brother and me that I'd pasted inside. He was just one week old, and I was cradling him carefully in my little five-year-old arms. He'd just returned from the hospital with my mother and was a curious bundle in a soft, light-blue blanket. I remember his delicate, downy, infant head and his squished, pink, baby face. It was a fond memory.

I flipped through the journal to the very last entry:

Nightmare. I'm with Jason, and we're in a busy mall. We become separated, and I realize my purse is gone. I have no wallet and no cell phone. A mall security guard stops to help me but asks for my passport. I try to explain to him I have no identification. I tell him to call my therapist… that she can prove who I am. He looks at me like I'm crazy.

Rodrigo came over and placed two plates of eggs and toast on the table, then went back into the kitchen and grabbed two forks. He sat down and took a big bite of toast. I leaned over and showed him my brother's picture.

"That was my brother. It's the only picture I have of him."

"You don't mention your family very much."

"They're all dead. My brother was the last of my family, and he died five years ago. It's just me."

"I'm sorry to hear that. I'd be lost without my family. It must have been tough for you."

That was the reason I didn't talk about my family. I hated people feeling sorry for me. I shrugged.

"It's okay. I don't like to dwell on the past. Dr. Serena says it's important to stay in the present moment."

"Speaking of which, my six-month contract is up in three weeks," he said.

My chest tightened. *So soon?* He was a traveling therapist and jumped at the chance to accept a six-month gig in California from Texas. We had been between jobs and relationships when we met five months ago. Neither of us tethered to anything or anyone. I'd been working part-time at an animal rescue non-profit. The charity offered me a fulltime job, but I wasn't ready for a forty-hour work week again. Before I'd gotten married, I had gotten laid off from an investment firm in San Francisco, but I'd salted away my three-month severance pay and cashed in my company stock. The funds were sitting in a money market fund.

"From the moment we met, I noticed this spiritual connection," Rodrigo continued. "I know we're soulmates and we've been together before."

"Maybe that's why the sex is so good," I joked. "But you're moving on to who-knows-where, and I'm at a crossroads too."

"I can re-up my contract."

"I thought you were looking at a contract in Hawaii?"

"I was, but that was before we met."

I wasn't ready for that. I was still processing my divorce, nearly a year now, and wasn't certain of being in another long-term relationship. Then Rodrigo and Markus popped up in my life simultaneously. Two totally different men. Rodrigo was so much younger, a soulful, determined, Capricorn, Hispanic/Portuguese male, and Markus—an older German business executive. Markus was another ambitious and simmering Scorpio man like my ex-husband.

As if reading my thoughts, Rodrigo asked, "So, what's up with this dude Markus?"

"What do you mean? I thought we set ground rules about this."

"Yeah, yeah, I know. I just didn't expect to get attached to you so quickly." He looked down at the dining table and seemed embarrassed.

This always happened to me. I met men who told me they just want something casual… then they got attached.

"I don't know about Markus," I said. "So far, we've just had some coffee dates. He travels a lot to different corporate offices. I haven't actually spent a lot of time with him."

"You know I'll always be there for you," Rodrigo said suddenly. "You believe me, right?"

I didn't comment. I just didn't trust people who made promises like that. Of course, I knew it had to do with my parents who abruptly vacated from my life when I was a child. As I got older, I just got better at keeping the ghosts at bay.

"I like what we have. I like being with you, but I'm still figuring out what's next."

He nodded. "I get that. I'm good with hanging out for now." He took my hand and kissed it.

"Let's just enjoy the moment okay?" I said.

The last I saw of Rodrigo, he was walking down the driveway. He turned and lifted his hand in a fond farewell.

The sunlight formed an unusually bright halo around him. He gave me his sweetest smile and climbed into his dark blue Mini Cooper. As he sped off, the song "Believer" by Imagine Dragons blasted from his car stereo.

Chapter Two

After I showered and tidied the kitchen, I got ready for my lunch date with my girlfriend, slipping into a short-sleeved navy jumpsuit with matching navy sandals. I grabbed my leather handbag and stepped outside.

My landlady, Lulu Woo, was spraying down the driveway in front the triplex I lived in. At almost six feet tall, she was an imposing figure in her fuchsia, Old Navy sweat suit and black, rubber flip flops. Her snowy hair was styled in a pixie cut, and her round face was lightly creased across her forehead. At seventy, she was in hearty shape, and I hoped I'd age as gracefully.

She greeted me warmly as I walked down the driveway. "Hey, I saw your cute boyfriend leaving," she winked at me. "Robbing the cradle… huh. *Aiya!*"

I blushed.

"You go girl. Enjoy your life… what are you doing today?"

"Therapy appointment and lunch with a girlfriend."

"You see that sex therapist right? The one who used to have an advice column in the paper?" She giggled.

"She's actually a marriage, family, and child counselor. She wrote the column a long time ago to market herself. I think she didn't have any clue how popular that blog was going to be!"

"Is she helping you get over your divorce? I hope so. He didn't deserve you, my dear. He took all that money from you and wasn't even grateful. Shameful."

She went back to hosing down the driveway as I got into my Honda CRV. I regretted having confided in Lulu. She'd been so warm and welcoming when I moved in, and my personal saga had spilled out over several cups of chamomile tea and her chocolate chip banana bread.

I hated talking about the divorce. I had been one of those starry-eyed women who truly believed we'd make it "until death do we part." Twenty years was a good run, but the unraveling of my marriage had crushed me

I was glad my therapist was still practicing, since she had helped me so much in the past.

The drive to her home was easy since she lived close by. Her large, cedar-shingled house came into view, and as always, I parked in her sloped driveway. As I walked up the terra cotta flagstones toward the back gate, I heard the pleasant sound of metal wind chimes and pushed the wooden gate open. The quaint, domed, white latticed gazebo came into view, her newly built office nestled snugly inside a small grove of redwood trees. Her contractor son had torn down the former tool shed, and it was now a whimsical space decorated with her treasured orchid plants and padded light brown wicker furniture.

Her black and white Tuxedo cat, Bast, was resting on one of the padded chairs. I walked up to him and stroked his soft head. He lifted it briefly in acknowledgement, then went back to ignoring me.

"You're early!"

I turned to see my therapist padding slowly across the flagstone path toward me. She'd always been a bit zaftig, but her slower gait was a result of hip replacement. As always, she was dressed fastidiously in an all-black ensemble—a loose fitting tunic top over black slacks and topped with a black gauzy silk jacket. She had on a fancy, black fascinator hat with black netting, which partially covered her forehead. Her pale, heart shaped face was made up simply with just mascara and red lipstick, her dark, wavy hair falling to her shoulders and her gray blue eyes fixed on me with amusement.

"You look glam… as always!" I said.

She sighed and lowered herself gingerly into a padded wicker chair, waving at Bast to get off the adjacent chair.

"I'm going to a funeral after our session," she responded. "Another one of my neighbors transitioned."

She said this calmly, and I was again reminded of her octogenarian status. It was hard to believe sometimes.

"How can I help you today?" She rested her hands on her lap.

"Rodrigo spent the night with me, and at breakfast, Markus called me."

She smiled. "Must have been awkward."

"Not really, I didn't pick up, and Rodrigo is pretty cool about it."

"But…"

I shrugged. "I've been above board with them both. In fact, they both told me they wanted a casual, *friends with benefits* type of arrangement. Then this morning, Rodrigo said he wanted to renew his contract to stay here. To be with me."

"How do you feel about that?"

"Confused. Like what the hell am I doing dating two men? Maybe I rushed into this too soon. Maybe I should be processing my divorce and all that."

"You *have* been processing your divorce… with *me*."

"I just don't want anyone to get hurt. I feel comfortable with Rodrigo, but I'm attracted to Markus. He's worldly, charming, and my own age—we have a lot more in common."

"You're overthinking all this. Can't you just enjoy being courted by two men. Why not just allow yourself to feel desirable again?"

I didn't have an answer, and as a strange anxiety bubbled up, I looked away from her and noticed a crystal vase with a tropical flower arrangement. Stems of brilliant red ginger stalks paired with colorful birds of paradise and white orchid blossoms created a pleasing bouquet. I still had a ridiculous hope that Jason would re-appear sober and chastened. That he would fight to win me back. Sometimes I felt like my dalliance with Rodrigo was just a distraction from facing the fact that Jason was really gone for good.

"I still have feelings for Jason," I said. I waited for my therapist to ridicule or chastise me.

"Of course, you do. You always will. I'm still close to my ex-husband. He's the father of my children, so we have that connection. I've told you before… people come into our life for a reason, a season, or a lifetime. Jason came for a season. Have you heard from him lately?"

I shook my head.

"Is your attorney still pursuing Jason about the loan?"

I nodded. I didn't want to talk about my divorce. I was tired of it. I was also upset at myself for letting my former husband pressure me into loaning him fifty thousand dollars from my trust to keep his restaurant afloat. Luckily, the trust's attorney insisted Jason sign a promissory note. It was even stipulated in the divorce filing that Jason pay me back within a year. Bupkis so far.

"Well, he needs to pay you back in full plus interest."

I looked up to see her stern expression.

"He promised you he'd pay you back, and he needs to keep his word."

"I know. He had to sell one of his cars to pay off his expenses, so I know he's hurting for cash."

"You're doing it again—making excuses for him." She said this calmly, but it felt like she was reprimanding me for being a gullible idiot.

Honestly, I just wanted it to be over with. I thought about asking him for his vintage 1966 Mustang convertible as payment in full since I was pretty sure his cash flow was non-existent. He already had a second car, an older Prius that belonged to his daughter that she dropped off before going back to college.

Owning an expensive car had never appealed to me, and it was ironic that at one point, Jason had offered to give me his BMW X1 as a wedding present. I always had a strong practical streak and was content to drive around in my old Honda CRV because I could haul my dog and bike in the back. However, now the dog had crossed the Rainbow Bridge, and my bike was gathering dust in a storage locker.

The bike had been a birthday gift from him, and I hadn't wanted it. It was a powder blue beach cruiser that cost two thousand dollars and I'd ridden it once. I'd asked him for a cheaper regular beach cruiser to ride around the neighborhood, but he got a souped up e-bike version that made me nervous because it went so fast. Plus, I was worried the lithium battery might blow up in our garage.

Aunt Lily had disapproved of Jason's lavish, exorbitant habits. Especially his penchant for expensive cars and watches. I was shocked how much his monthly car payments were on his Mercedes SUV and how much he paid for his Coppard opal gold watch. In the beginning, his extravagant spending had been thrilling to experience. It was a stark contrast to my upbringing, which had been spent religiously clipping coupons for groceries and not eating out.

I was disappointed in myself for breaking a promise to my aunt. The trust fund money she left me was salted away until I turned sixty-five. The attorney who managed the trust reluctantly let me withdraw some money on an emergency basis to cover Jason's payroll for one month. I sat in his spartan law office, I knew I was making a mistake. I could see Aunt Lilly's disapproving visage in my head. I could hear her accusing voice telling me how men were greedy, sex-driven cretins. She never married and worked hard to take care of me, working two jobs and denying herself any extravagances.

Now Dr. Serena was reminding me of that transaction.

"I'm so glad your attorney insisted on the promissory note. Now you just have to go to court and make sure he pays up."

"It's not as easy as that. My divorce attorney would have to file paperwork at the courthouse so that the sheriff could collect the money. From what she said, serving divorce papers is a low priority for the sheriff's department. She even said Jason could make payments. But so far… *nothing*."

"I know it's hard for you to let go. But… the way this works is that you have to *believe* it'll happen. You also have to trust that the universe has your back and will deliver. Remember, life is happening for you and not to you."

I didn't respond. It seemed like I got this criticism over and over… how I was stuck in the past.

"There's a part of you still corded to him energetically. Have you been doing the cord cutting exercises I told you about? It's time to let him go."

Tears suddenly formed in my eyes.

"I can't… I know he's struggling right now."

She leaned over and pushed a box of tissues toward me.

"Yes, he *is* struggling. He made his choice—he could have stepped up and been the partner you deserve. But he didn't."

I dabbed a wadded-up tissue to my eyes. I didn't know how she could expect me to process a twenty-year marriage so quickly. She'd been the one to insist I get out and circulate to meet men and have fun. At eighty years old, she'd had three husbands and made an amazing life for herself through her successful psychotherapy practice.

"Are you writing in your journal?"

I shook my head.

"I need to start again."

"How's your sweet friend Kailani? You haven't mentioned her in a while."

"We talk every week. She wants me to come out for a visit soon."

"I remember my time in the islands with my second husband. Such a magical place. He once told me he came from a family of shapeshifters—that his beloved uncle was the family aumakua. He told me crazy stories about his uncle shapeshifting into a reef shark and watching over them!"

She chuckled.

"You were married to a Hawaiian? You never mentioned it."

"I'm sure you met Nakoa at my annual Christmas party. He comes every year.

I vaguely recalled a dark-skinned, elegant looking man with thick coal-black shoulder length hair.

"I do remember. I just thought he was one of your neighbors."

"I think you should go visit Kai and explore your heritage. I feel the islands are summoning you to return."

"I've always felt rooted here. I don't feel a connection to the islands. I love visiting but San Francisco's always been my home."

Dr. Serena reached over and fondly patted my knee.

"There's so much for you to discover. Have you ever heard of the mo'o? They are female shapeshifters who transform from maidens into water dragons. Nakoa used to tell all kinds of wonderful stories from his childhood. It's part of your heritage…it's who you are."

Before I could comment, I heard the doorbell ring inside the house. Dr. Serena stood up slowly.

"My next client is here."

We ended the session with our customary hug. As I walked down the path toward my car, I wondered what prompted her fanciful musing. I also pondered over the strange coincidence that she had actually lived in the islands.

Chapter Three

I've always loved the drive to Jason's former restaurant. I hopped on 101 Southbound, and traffic flowed smoothly, then I took the main exit toward Tiburon. Within moments, I was rewarded with a stunning view across the bay of the town of Sausalito, with the Golden Gate Bridge in the distance. The gently undulating waves of the Pacific Ocean shimmered like silvery fish scales in the brilliant sunlight.

I pulled over at the next pull out to snap a picture with my phone, getting out of the car and standing silently as I took in the gently undulating sun-dappled waves. An intense longing overcame me, and I had this overwhelming urge to jump into the water. I sighed and shook myself—what a crazy thought!

When I pulled into the modest parking lot downtown across from the restaurant, I saw my girlfriend's black Cadillac Escalade SUV parked near the front. There was a Keep Tahoe Blue sticker on her bumper. I got out and stood across the street from the restaurant.

I had so many good memories of Jason and me sitting on the spacious wooden deck overlooking the ocean, enjoying cocktails. It was our second home, and the restaurant staff was our family. I understood why Jason left town after he and his business partner sold the restaurant. It'd been a huge part of our lives and his consuming passion for ten years.

Cassie Lopez was already seated at a prime table on the large deck. She was dressed in a racer back, pale pink and black floral tennis dress and black Nike tennis shoes. The dress looked a bit snug, and her most distinguishing feature—her ample bosom—seemed ready to pop out of the top. Her face was partially hidden behind tortoise shell Prada sunglasses, but I could see tear stains on her puffy cheeks.

"Hey!" I said. "Are you okay?"

She glanced up from her menu and sighed. "He signed the papers."

I was flummoxed. Then a light came on. *The divorce papers?*

"The divorce papers," she repeated and took out a tissue from her handbag and dabbed at her face.

"Well, isn't that what you've been waiting for?"

She blew her nose. "Of course, I have!"

Cassie was the first one to admit she had first world problems. Her grandparents came over the border from Mexico and sacrificed everything for Cassie's mother, an only child. She grew up in SoCal, mainly in Santa Barbara, with a successful Irish-Catholic accountant father, and her mother was a pampered stay-at-home housewife. It seemed predestined that Cassie would marry a successful accountant and become a pampered housewife herself.

"So, you got the house, right?"

"Yep and the cabin in Tahoe."

She went back to staring at the Pescion Cafe menu even though she always ordered the same thing every time—the catch of the day with a glass of chilled Chardonnay. Her favorite waiter, Jonas, came over and greeted us. Jonas had been a longtime fixture at the cafe, having recently celebrated twenty years at the restaurant. He was tall and lean with a shaved head and graying goatee—he always knew how to charm Cassie to ensure a generous tip.

"Good afternoon, ladies. How are my favorite customers?"

He put down two glasses of ice water and gazed fondly at Cassie, who enjoyed his attention. She flipped her sunglasses on top of her head and fluttered her eyelashes at him.

"Chardonnay for Miss Cassie and Arnold Palmer for my hula girl?" he teased.

"What's good today, Jonas?" Cassie asked with a smile.

"We got fresh halibut with a mushroom risotto and sautéed spinach."

Cassie paused and blurted out, "I'm going to do the fish and chips!"

Jonas and I exchanged surprised looks.

"I'll have the halibut," I said. He nodded cheerfully and took away our menus.

"You never eat fried foods!" I exclaimed.

Cassie sighed. "I know… it's my cheat day. I'm going to have the butterscotch cake too."

"You should be celebrating. He signed the papers—you can move on finally!"

She took a sip of her ice water and shrugged. "I thought I'd feel relieved, but I just feel… *empty*."

I nodded sympathetically, remembering how anti-climactic it had been when I received the final divorce documents. I'd been pretty numb during the entire divorce process. It was a form of self-preservation I'd developed as a child, putting my feelings on hold until the crisis passed and self-medicating with junk food like double decker chocolate moon pies. I'd binge on moon pies during my menstrual cycle or during school finals. Jason had bought me a case off Amazon for me when I'd had surgery to remove an ovarian cyst years ago. It was still my go-to comfort snack when I wanted to be soothed.

Jonas returned with our drinks, and we clinked glasses.

"So, you and Isabella still into the pickleball? Your tennis dress is cute!"

She rolled her eyes. "That kid is driving me nuts. Thank God her father has her this weekend. She's like the Energizer Bunny… at least she has an outlet for all that energy. And you won't believe this…Steve took her to Vegas for a family reunion and now she wants to be a mermaid!"

"I'm not following."

"There's an actual mermaid show at a casino and now she wants to get a mermaid tail and swim underwater with fish. Then my abuela gets on the bandwagon because she swears that Celestina told her she used to be a mermaid in a past life. According to my grandmother, when Celestina was five, she told her that she used to live underwater in a magical city."

"You mean like in the Aquaman movie?"

"Something like that. My grandmother claims she took Celestina to the beach once and Celestina told her *I belong in the ocean.*"

Cassie's story stirred something inside me. A brief, flickering memory of my mother and me at a beach in Hawaii. Her loving smile as she caressed my hair and pointed at the ocean.

"Hello…Earth to Noel. Where'd you go?"

Cassie's voice startled me.

"Sorry. I thought you said you had a past life reading once?"

"Oh…*that*. What a waste of money. I didn't expect to be Cleopatra or anything but the psychic blathered on about Steve and me having several lives together. She said we were even brother and sister once. *Yuck!*"

"Don't feel bad. I got a reading when Jason and I were having problems. The psychic said we were mother and son once and that Jason had stolen money from me and I'd cut him out of my will. Now…*that's weird.* She also said he might be keeping something from me. Something important."

"Like what…a second wife stashed somewhere?"

"Knowing Jason…probably back taxes. He always filed extensions."

"If you signed off on the returns, you're on the hook if he owes the IRS money!"

Cassie's eyes widened with alarm. My stomach clenched up. The old Jason would have fastidiously filed our taxes on time. Now I wasn't so sure. I pushed the worrisome thought aside and changed the subject.

"Hey, I meant to ask how your Cabo vacation went with Montrell."

"Montrell and I over-indulged when we were in Cabo. We always go to Panchos and get the ribs, and those margaritas went down easy!"

I remembered all her Instagram pictures of her Cabo trip—including the one of her slamming back a shot of rattlesnake tequila.

"I saw your pictures… was that snake dead inside the tequila jar? That was kinda freaky," I said.

She giggled and got that bad girl glint in her eyes. "Of course, it was dead. It was pickled in alcohol. And in case you're wondering, there's no venom in it."

As I was about to respond, I heard a familiar voice and looked up to see my ex-husband's former business partner, Candace Love. I was startled, and my stomach knotted up for no obvious reason.

"Hey, lady, long time no see!" Candace stood over me, dressed in the restaurant's server uniform—a starched, white, long-sleeved cotton shirt over black trousers. Over her outfit, she wore a navy-blue fleece pullover jacket with the restaurant's logo—a leaping, smiling salmon with a white chef's hat. At sixty, she looked pretty good, with short-cropped platinum blonde hair and her signature glossy plum lipstick.

I stood up and we exchanged air kisses on each cheek. "This is my friend, Cassie."

Candace nodded while Cassie acknowledged her with a finger wave.

"I'm surprised you're still around. I thought you'd take the money and take off for Cabo," I said.

"Yeah, well, plans change… life happens, right? Remember my Frenchie dog? He needed surgery to fix his hip dysplasia. Four thousand out the door. Besides, I'm so damned attached to this place, and the tips are pretty decent on the weekends. So, there you go."

"I don't suppose Jason's been around?" I asked.

She shrugged. "I ran into him maybe last month at the farmers market."

I had the strong sense she was lying.

Jonas returned with our drinks.

"I better get busy, enjoy your lunch!" Candace chirped. She nodded at Jonas and left.

"Jonas, have you seen Jason around lately?"

He busied himself putting paper coasters on the table. "Sure, he was here the other day. I guess he can't stay away—like Candace." He chuckled. "We're like a family here. We just have new parents, right?"

He scurried away as Cassie and I sipped our drinks, and absorbing what Jonas just said, my skin got clammy. *Jason was back in California.*

"Are you okay?" Cassie asked.

"Just surprised he's back."

"Did Candace and Jason ever hook up? She sure acted funny."

"Maybe before I met him. But he swears they were strictly business partners."

I had noticed in the past how Candace would talk affectionately about my ex-husband. I even caught her touching him when they were together working. Little things—like resting her head on his shoulder, putting her arm around his waist, and rubbing his back. Even worse, Candace's constant texts every single day. There was always some restaurant crisis she needed Jason to resolve. I didn't like it and even brought it up with him, but he insisted it was all business related. I believed him because we had a healthy sex life. Besides, he put in arduous hours at the restaurant and would come home exhausted. Now… I wondered.

"Well, it's water under the bridge!" Cassie said. She lifted her wine glass up in a toast. "To new beginnings."

"Onward and upward!" I agreed.

But I wished I could ignore that disquieting feeling I had in my gut.

Chapter Four

I drove home in a pensive mood. It always felt like things happened to me in sixes not threes. Major changes seemed to erupt randomly in my life, such as my recent divorce. Besides the divorce, I'd gotten laid off from my job, and my car got totaled by a drunk driver.

As I pulled into the driveway, I noticed Lulu's white Toyota Prius was gone. After I parked, I went around back to my in-law unit, and Lulu had left me cookies in a sealed, teal Tupperware bowl on my doorstep. I lifted the lid, and the pleasing aroma of cinnamon drifted out. I loved her Snickerdoodle cookies and made a mental note to text her later.

Opening my front door and stepping inside, the soothing scent of lavender hung in the air. I liked to diffuse essential oils to make my apartment feel homey. I'd lived in this apartment for almost a year, and yet when I walked in, it still felt like someone else's home. My soul hadn't landed yet.

I took in the tidy apartment decorated in pleasant neutrals. The space was painted a warm beige and was small and narrow, like living in an RV, with walnut hardwood floors. Lulu had furnished it tastefully, with a caramel leather loveseat and two matching poufs that served as a coffee table.

My tiny kitchen was also courtesy of Ikea; butcher block counters, pale gray cabinets, with a darker gray subway tiled backsplash. I had stainless steel appliances, and my own decorating touch was two plastic bride and groom Norfin troll dolls that Jason had gifted me on our wedding day and a framed refrigerator magnet of my former dog. I had sold or given everything away after the divorce.

I put down my purse on one of the poufs and flopped down on the loveseat. I loved my place, but I sorely missed my spacious, old, pine-green kitchen with the big, white, ceramic farmhouse sink and customized blue, Mexican, tiled counter.

I was in an odd sentimental mood as I thought about Celestina's mermaid story. I used to have an old photograph of my mother and me at the beach when I was about four years old. It was the only keepsake I'd hung onto all these years and the only picture I had of my mother. I wondered where that photo was?

I went into the bedroom and rummaged in the back of the closet. There was a cardboard bankers box that I'd used to stash some legal documents from my Aunt Lilly's estate. I removed the lid and looked inside and sifted through some large manila mailing envelopes. One envelope wasn't labeled and felt heavy. I turned the envelope upside down and emptied the contents. A few black and white photographs spilled out. Then I found it. I stared at the grainy photograph of my mother and me. *We belong in the ocean.*

There was a knock at the door, and I got up, expecting to see Lulu as I opened it. Instead, to my shock, Jason was standing there. My mouth fell open, and a chill shivered over me as goosebumps rippled down both arms.

"What're you doing here?" I blurted.

"Nice to see you too."

He appeared to have dropped some weight, but he looked good. He had that same roguish smile and wore his customary aviator sunglasses, which always made him look dashing. He forked his fingers through his reddish auburn hair and cleared his throat.

"This a bad time?"

Was there ever a good time to run into a former spouse? I stood back from the doorway, and he pressed past me. He was wearing a black and white cube printed silk shirt over faded jeans and a black leather aviator jacket.

"You still have those loafers!" I said.

He looked down at the slip-on black suede loafers that had seen better days. "They're *comfortable!*" He surveyed my apartment. "Cute."

I shut the door and tried to process the fact that my former husband was inside my apartment after not seeing him for almost a year. A strange mixture of disbelief, irritation, and nervousness permeated my body. I crossed my arms over my chest.

"What are you doing here?"

"Mind if I have a glass of water?" he asked. He moved toward the kitchen and retrieved a water glass from the sink, rinsed it out, and filled it with tap water. He nodded at the reverse osmosis filter. "Good call. Makes the water taste better."

"You can thank my landlady."

He nodded and slurped the entire glass down, then refilled it and moved over to my loveseat, taking off his sunglasses and resting them on one of the leather poufs.

I sat down on a pouf facing him, that familiar, visceral reaction when he was near me rearing its head. In the beginning, it made for great sex, but now it was nerve-wracking and uncomfortable.

"You look amazing," Jason said. His eyes swept over me, and much to my annoyance, I was getting turned on. A primal heat flooded me.

A spontaneous memory of us sweaty and intertwined popped into my head, the scent of his musky aftershave, the taste of his insistent tongue in my mouth all flooding my senses.

"Why are you here?" I asked.

"I wanted to see you, I missed you."

"You could have called first."

"I wasn't sure if you'd answer."

"I probably wouldn't have."

The sensual thoughts continued. The memory of his hands caressing my nipples, the first time he slid his tongue *down there*.

"You have every right to be angry."

"Gee, thanks. I feel so much better now that I have your approval."

He got up and leaned in close to me. His breath was minty, and his hazel eyes locked onto mine. I wanted to jump his bones. That's how it always happened with us—huge fights followed by insane sex to release pent-up tension.

I took a step back. If he kissed me, the dam would break, and I'd let him have his way with me. My rational brain was screaming, *"No!"* but my primitive animal self was screaming, *"Yes!"*

He stroked my upper arm lightly with the back of his hand, testing me. Ripples of goosebumps fanned all over my body. He moved in closer, and I knew I'd let him kiss me. I backed away quickly."

"You lost weight," I said.

"I quit drinking and joined a program."

"*You did?*"

"I suppose that's partially why I'm here—to make amends."

I didn't know how to respond. I thought about all those times when he drank himself silly and I had pleaded with him to join a program. The moments when I'd driven late at night to pick him up from the restaurant when he'd call me, his words slurred and unintelligible. His bitchiness when he woke up with a screaming hangover the next day. It soon became obvious that his drinking was more important than saving our marriage.

"You really got clean and sober?"

"Why is that so hard to believe?"

Then there was another knock at the front door. I snapped out of my trance and went to open the door. It was Rodrigo.

"Hey, babe!" He was still in his pale blue hospital scrubs and was holding a large cardboard pizza box. "I had a cancellation, so thought I'd bop over. Is something wrong?" He looked over my shoulder. "You've got company?"

"He's about to leave," I replied.

I was surprised how calm I sounded. Rodrigo moved past me and went straight to the kitchen. He put the pizza box on the counter, turned around, and stuck his hand out at Jason.

"Rodrigo… you must be Jason."

Talk about when worlds collide. I was watching a French rom com! My face was hot, but the heat emanating between my legs still pulsed intensely. Jason stood and shook hands with Rodrigo. I went over and stood next to Rodrigo, and he slipped his arm around my shoulders.

"Well, this is a bit awkward," Jason said. He grabbed his sunglasses and moved toward the front door. As he was retreating, Rodrigo said forcefully, "Hey, bro'… when are you going to pay her back the fifty grand?"

Jason stopped at the door with his hand on the handle, tossing over his shoulder, "That's why I came by today. To talk about that—I'll call you later."

Then he slipped out and shut the door quietly. I looked at Rodrigo and put my hand on his chest. "Give me a moment."

I hurried outside just as Jason got into his BMW. "Jason."

He was sitting down but looked up at me.

"Why are you here? It's been a whole year, and you just want to pop back into my life out of nowhere?" I hadn't meant to sound so shrill and angry, but there it was. I liked being in control of my feelings but realized it was a lost cause.

"I want you back."

I stared at him blankly. *What the hell was he thinking? Did he think I was sitting around pining for him the past year? How could he be so arrogant?*

"Your lover boy seems nice," Jason said.

"Rodrigo *is* nice. He's been really good to me."

"I'm glad. You deserve that."

We both fell silent, not knowing what else to say. I started to walk away when he called out.

"Meet me for dinner."

I kept walking.

***

Rodrigo was the happy beneficiary of all the bottled up sexual energy that Jason provoked. When I got back inside, I grabbed him and kissed him forcefully. He moaned and gripped my butt and started kneading roughly. We stumbled into the bedroom, where I pushed him down on the bed and stripped off his pants and boxer shorts.

I took him into my mouth, and he gasped loudly, then I yanked off my top and bra and sat on him as he buried his face between my breasts. He flipped me over on my back to tug my leggings and panties off and in an instant entered me with a groan. I shut my eyes and imagined it was Jason, climaxing violently. Then he arched his back up slightly and exploded inside me.

***

"Your ex-husband needs to stop by more often," Rodrigo joked. We were lying in bed after gobbling up the extra-large meat pizza he'd brought by. The smell of garlic, pepperoni, and green bell peppers still permeated the kitchen. I snuggled next to him and inhaled sandalwood soap off his skin.

"That was so hot the way he got you riled up. *Woof*," he chuckled.

"You're not jealous?

"Are you kidding? He's out there getting shit-faced because he didn't get to have you, and I'm here enjoying the goods."

"Thanks for not getting upset. You handled it so well." I snuggled closer to him, and he automatically leaned over and kissed me on the top of my head.

"What did you ever see in him?"

I sighed. "He was different when we met. Things changed after the pandemic, and he lost the restaurant. Then his mother almost died from Covid, and his drinking was out of control."

My voice trailed off. Our marriage had hit an all-time low, but I'd been sure we'd get through it. We'd rallied through other marital slumps. Yet, somehow, I'd known something was really off. I just didn't want to believe it.

Rodrigo threaded his fingers through mine. "I just don't want him to hurt you again. You stuck with him through thick and thin, and then he ghosts you and didn't even try to pay the money back. Very *lame*."

His caring touched me, and I sat up and kissed him.

"I'm ready for round two," I said.

Chapter Five

I had that sinking feeling again about my life happening in sixes. I was sitting at Lulu's pine kitchen table, watching her pour jasmine tea into delicate porcelain teacups. She had an impressive tea seat, with an oblong upright teapot, sugar bowl, and creamer. The pattern was a colorful floral design, with a gold background and Asian motif edging around the rim of the teacups. She served pumpkin spice muffins on a plain, white, bone china dinner plate. I bit into a warm pumpkin muffin that Lulu had lavished a generous dollop of butter on. Nirvana.

"I have an announcement to make." Lulu was dressed in a navy-blue, flowing, Hawaiian muumuu dress with a bold floral print of pink orchids and green palm fronds. "I'm selling the house," she said.

I said nothing as a queasy sensation bubbled inside my stomach.

"My daughter's going to have another baby, and she needs me back in Honolulu."

I devoured the muffin and took a sip of tea. The fragrant jasmine scent was soothing.

"When is this happening?" I asked finally.

"I called my girlfriend, who's a realtor, and she agreed to come over this week. I'll probably have to clean everything out and get it staged."

"You don't want to keep the place and rent it out?"

"To be honest, I need the money. I've almost paid off the mortgage, and with this market, who knows what'll happen?" She carefully buttered a muffin and sighed. "I feel Madame Pele calling me home."

She was referring to the volcano goddess Pele. Some people felt a strong connection to her and could sense the volcanic rumblings in advance. "I was on the big island during the last eruption. I saw the white dog days before, so *I knew* it was coming." Lulu said this calmly with conviction. "You don't believe me?"

"I've heard rumors that Pele sends her big white dog to warn the locals. Mysterious things happen on the islands," I agreed. "When Jason and I honeymooned there, we were snorkeling on the North Shore. Somehow, we got separated, and I freaked out a little. Then this big turtle swam up to me. I was so surprised that I forgot all about Jason!" I chuckled at the memory.

"I saw your man this morning. He looked pretty happy driving away!" She winked at me. "Who was that man that stopped by yesterday afternoon? Was that your ex-husband?"

"Yep, that was Jason."

"So, now you're going out with another man tonight? Who is *that?*"

"Markus. I met him at the gym. We chatted a few times and bonded over our mutual divorces."

Lulu clicked her tongue. "All these men… so little time!" she joked.

"*I know*. It's nice to be sought after. I didn't realize how badly my self-esteem had suffered at the end. The last year, when Jason came home late at night, he'd crash on the living room sofa. We didn't even talk throughout the whole divorce process. We just communicated through our attorneys."

I recalled the lonely, sleepless nights when I heard the front door open. I'd sit up expectantly, waiting for Jason to come into the bedroom. Instead, I'd hear him in the guest bathroom showering and then in the kitchen, opening and closing the refrigerator. He didn't even look in on me like he used to. We'd become total strangers.

Now I was dating two different men and trying to feel better about myself. Markus had called earlier and left a voicemail. He was in town and wanted to take me out to dinner in Sausalito. My life was getting too complicated—I was happy with Rodrigo, and I only agreed to dinner with Markus because I enjoyed our insightful and flirty conversations at the gym. Thankfully, there was no word from Jason.

"I'm glad I never got married. I enjoy my freedom too much." Lulu dabbed her mouth daintily with a paper napkin. "I want to add a clause as a condition of the house sale that you can stay on as a tenant. I'm not sure how that works, I'll have to check with my realtor. I don't want you to worry about anything."

My eyes grew moist, deeply touched that she wanted to take care of me.

***

Markus pulled up promptly at six-thirty in his light-gray Volvo sedan. I was sitting outside on the wrought iron garden bench when I heard the gate latch jingle. I never knew what to wear on a casual date. I usually defaulted to a simple, sleeveless, black dress and accessorized it with bright colors. But I couldn't figure out how to make a black outfit chic without looking like I was going to a funeral. Courtesy of Lulu last Christmas, I had a fuchsia wool wrap with white edging to brighten my outfit. A fuchsia leather clutch bag, black beaded earrings, and black leather sandals completed my look. I'd dabbed on some tuberose perfume oil at the last minute.

Markus looked even more like a college professor in his gray, plaid, wool blazer over a gray collared shirt and wingtip leather shoes. He was brandishing a bouquet of peach-colored garden roses wrapped in brown paper with matching peach, satin ribbons. When I stood up, he leaned over and kissed my cheek.

"These had your name on it." He presented me the bouquet with a shy smile.

"Thank you so much."

"You look amazing."

"Thank you. Do you mind if I run inside and put these in the sink?"

He gestured toward the front door. I hurried in, found a glass pitcher, and filled it with water, sticking the flowers into the pitcher and turning to see him hovering in the doorway.

"Would you like to come in? Or do we need to get going?"

He glanced down at his watch. It was a stylish fashion watch with a black dial and black leather wristband.

"I'm afraid with traffic, we should get going. Maybe later?" He smiled. The suggestive remark hung in the air between us.

What was I thinking?

***

"Is the music okay?"

Markus had put on his favorite jazz playlist and the song "Patricia" by Art Pepper. The vibrant sound of Pepper's alto saxophone filled the car.

"I like this. Funny enough, it was a TV show that introduced me to Art Pepper."

"A TV show?" Markus looked puzzled.

"It was a detective show based in Los Angeles. I even bought the soundtrack."

He nodded but made no comment as we both basked silently in the lovely song. The drive to Sausalito didn't take long as we sped down Highway 101 south. We parked in the public lot on Bridgeway, a finger of silvery gray fog hovering over the Bay in the distance.

Markus got out first, went around to my side, and opened my door, extending his hand to help me out. I was touched by this chivalrous gesture. We entered Poggio's Italian restaurant and waited by the bar as Markus let the host know we'd arrived.

It was a place I'd been to before but not in a long time. It was right in the middle of downtown Sausalito in the heavily trafficked tourist area, which I generally avoided. The cavernous dining room décor had dark wood paneling with parquet wood floors that gave the room a rustic feel.

"Markus!" The man at the host stand greeted Markus warmly with a clap on the shoulder.

"Noel, this is my good friend Scott. He manages this place." Markus said.

Scott clasped my hand in his with a warm squeeze. He was a sturdily built and portly man in his mid-fifties.

"Markus and I go way back." He gestured for us to follow him as he grabbed two menus, then sat us at a window table overlooking the busy street and placed the menus on the table with a flourish.

"Is this acceptable, Markus?"

"It's perfect. Thanks."

Scott nodded at me. "Blake will be with you to take your drink orders."

Blake? My stomach clenched nervously. What were the chances that it was the same Blake that was Jason's former employee?

"Noel, *babe*!"

I looked up to see the very same Blake beaming down at me. He was Jason's former assistant general manager at his restaurant.

I'd forgotten how incestuous the local restaurant business was. I stood, and we exchanged a quick hug as Markus looked on quizzically.

Blake was as handsome as ever. He was in his mid-thirties with a lean face, wavy, shoulder-length, coppery-brown hair, and deep, aquamarine eyes. He was dressed in the restaurant uniform made up of a crisp, white, long-sleeved shirt, black slacks, and black leather shoes.

"Markus, this is my friend Blake."

They shook hands. Before I could think of what to say next, Blake leaned over and put his hand on my shoulder affectionately.

"Noel is my workout client."

"You're a personal trainer?" Markus asked.

Blake nodded. "She's the most dedicated client I have. And… the *nicest*!"

I wasn't sure if Blake was playing up his gayness to reassure Markus or he was just being himself. He went on smoothly to say, "What can I bring you to drink?"

"Could you please give us a few more minutes?" I asked.

"Absolutely." Blake winked at me and hurried off. I hoped my red face didn't give away how awkward I felt. However, I was relieved Blake hadn't mentioned Jason or the restaurant. Cardinal rule number one when you're dating post-divorce is to not dwell on your ex-spouse. If Markus noticed my discomfort, he didn't comment. Instead, he perused the wine list intently.

"What are you thinking?" I asked.

"I'm feeling like a nice, chilled Chardonnay."

I was totally ignorant of wine pairings and wasn't sure if white wine even went with pasta. I would've guessed a red would be more complementary, but in the past, I'd relied on Jason's expertise, since he was a sommelier. I wondered faintly what he'd recommend?

I was checking out the dinner menu—I always got the seafood risotto, but the vegetarian linguini sounded good too. As if reading my mind, Markus picked up the dinner menu.

"What looks good to you?" he asked.

"Risotto. What about you? The last time I was here, I had pasta, and it was excellent."

"So I've heard."

"I was here with my bestie a while back. It was our weekly girl's night out."

Blake re-appeared suddenly like a genie from a bottle, bearing a breadbasket of sliced sourdough, butter, and fried risotto balls, which he put in the center of the table.

"Compliments of the manager. Are you ready to order?"

Markus asked for a wine recommendation.

"If you're both doing pasta, I'd go for the *Far Niente* from Napa. It's our top seller and my personal favorite. Really nice melon and citrus overtones. I know that girlfriend here loves the risotto… sooooo."

Markus glanced over at me. Blake had recommended the most expensive chardonnay on the wine list.

"That sounds good," I said. Markus ordered the clam fettucine, and Blake scooped up our menus.

Markus grew suddenly quiet and stared pensively at the risotto balls.

"Everything okay?" I asked.

He grimaced and sighed. "This has been weighing heavily on my mind."

My heart leapt. *Is he breaking up with me already? What is going on?*

"I'm not good at this midlife dating thing. I also feel self-conscious because I'm so much older than you," he blurted.

"I'm fifty-five."

"*Really?*" He laughed with relief. "So, I'm only five years older than you? I thought you were much younger."

"Dating hasn't been easy for me either. I'm pretty introverted, and my divorce only finalized six months ago."

"You don't act like an introvert. In fact, you seem warm and vivacious."

"I'm faking it," I joked. "Honestly, I wouldn't be putting myself out there if my therapist hadn't forced me."

"Then I'm glad she did. I was very nervous when I approached you at the gym. I felt utterly ridiculous."

"Really? You seemed pretty confident."

He shook his head. "I'd seen you at the gym for weeks, and it took all my courage to finally say something to you."

"I'm glad you did." I recalled our first meeting. I'd recently re-joined the gym only because they had such a nice indoor pool. After I'd done my laps, I'd gone down to the lobby and treated myself to a green smoothie and saw Markus lounging nearby at small table reading the New York Times. He was dressed in a stylish, dark-gray, camo hoodie over gray sweatpants and black running shoes. I recognized him from the pool, but we'd always just missed each other. I'd be arriving and he'd be leaving… or vice versa. There was an attractive stillness about him, and when he looked up from the newspaper and smiled at me, I had been smitten.

We'd chatted briefly and made a coffee date for the next day. Then a casual lunch date followed after that, where we'd shared our post-divorce details. He'd been married thirty years to his college sweetheart and had a daughter in college at UCLA. His wife had filed for divorce after confessing to an affair with a co-worker. I told him about Jason's restaurant floundering, his heavy drinking, and his mother's chronic health problems.

Now, Blake returned with the wine and filled our wine glasses. Markus raised his glass in a toast. "To new beginnings."

We clinked wineglasses, and I knew it would be a fine evening.

***

I went up to the ladies' room upstairs above the restaurant in the mezzanine. When I finished my business and walked outside to the parlor area, I saw Blake hurrying up the stairs toward me.

"Hey, cutie pie!"

We embraced in warm hug. "How's the date going? He's a hottie—got that sexy college professor vibe going!"

"He's an executive at a big investment firm," I said. "And… thanks for not mentioning Jason."

"So, he believed my bluff about being your personal trainer?"

I laughed. "That was inspired thinking. But it was partially true, since we do go to the same gym and workout sometimes."

"You heard from Jason at all?"

I sighed. "He actually popped up at my apartment the other day. Totally out of the blue and shocked me and Rodrigo."

"Oh my God. What *happened*?"

I gave him a quick rundown.

"Geez… talk about awkward. I'm with Rodrigo, though… give me my damn money back *asshole*!"

"When did you start working here? Why'd you leave the restaurant? I was just there, and they put some serious money into the renovation."

Blake rolled his eyes. "I don't do corporate. The first thing they did was stop comping the employee meals."

"*What?*"

"Yeah, and now the managers have to pay for their own parking. I was like… *fuck that*! Cheap ass bullshit. One night, Scott stopped by for a drink, and I told him I was thinking of jumping ship, and he offered me a job as a server. I want to travel again, so I said *hell yeah*. I heard half the staff quit."

I shook my head in surprise. "Jason would have hated being under the corporate thumb. The only thing I'd heard was he moved back to Seattle. After I filed, he went radio silent. Our attorneys did all the communicating."

Blake draped his arm around my shoulders. "Sorry, babe. You were too good to him. I know what a narcissist he could be. I'm glad you're moving on."

"Am I? Sometimes I wake up and still expect to feel him next to me. For some reason, I thought he'd snap out of his funk and we'd go back to the way it was. Sleeping in on Sundays, breakfast in bed… shopping at the farmers market."

"You're doing the right thing. When my father left, my mother she went into a massive depression. Never got over the divorce. I don't want that to happen to you. You deserve better. The fucking nerve of Jason to show up like that shows he hasn't changed. He took you for granted."

I didn't respond right away. I appreciated Blake's caring, but I didn't feel like talking about my divorce any further.

"I better get back to Markus. Thanks for stopping and saying hello. I've missed you. I guess I'll see you at the gym then?"

"You didn't hear? The gym got sold and they're getting rid of the pool. A huge bummer—I know you love to swim."

"*No pool?*"

"There's only one other gym with a pool across town."

"I guess I'll see you there, then?"

"You got it!"

We hugged once more, and I wondered if Markus thought I'd vanished into the ether.

***

We drove home listening to Ron Carter's "Light Blue," his mellow bass music the perfect way to end the evening. There was no traffic on the highway, and within minutes we were parked in front of Lulu's house.

"Thank you for a lovely evening," I said.

"I enjoyed it as well."

Markus had such a kind face. His soft gaze and low, gentle voice made him incredibly attractive to me. Yet something had been bothering me, and I needed to be honest with him, since he'd been forthright with me.

"I hope I'm not being presumptuous, but right now, I feel all I can offer is friendship. I don't want to waste your time or play games. I like you, but my life is unsettled, so I hope you understand."

"I appreciate your candor. It's refreshing." He reached for my hand and kissed it. "I did tell you that I'm unsure about dating or even steady companionship. I travel extensively for my job, and I know that contributed to my marriage collapsing. I'm in the process of changing careers, so there's a lot of moving parts."

"You're quitting your job?"

"It's a long story. I was offered a consulting position by a former colleague. It would mean less money, but I can make my own hours. I could spend more time with my son and even take a long, much needed vacation. Maybe I'll go lie on a beach in Hawaii for a month!" he joked. "I've got a nice rental in Maui, if you're ever interested."

"That's kind of you."

"I've got a place in Tahoe, too. It sits empty most of the time—I should sell it, but I bought it right after I got married. A lot of good memories there," he sighed.

"Well, I know you have a busy day, so I'll let you go."

I started to get out of the car, but he got out first and opened the passenger door for me, holding out his hand and pulling me to my feet. We stood facing each other in the quiet night, then he leaned over and kissed my cheek. His citrus aftershave smelled nice. I got on my tiptoes and kissed him lightly on the lips.

"Good night, Markus."

We silently walked up to my front door.

"Until next time," he said, and kissed the back of my hand sweetly. I fished for my front door key and turned back to see Markus pulling away into the night. I wondered if I'd see him again. There was a lot to think about.

Chapter Six

In the dream, I'm paddling a kayak in the ocean and I look up to see a huge tidal wave cresting toward me. I am frozen in fear and realize futilely I can't escape being swept away as it barrels ominously toward me. I hear my mother's voice calling out to me: "it's all right…don't be afraid." Miraculously, I am intact, bobbing along the waves. My kayak is gone but it feels liberating to float freely. A spinner dolphin surfaces next to me and I sense that it wants me to swim along. As it submerges deep into the ocean, I realize with a burst of joy that I can keep up as it dives farther and farther down. I wonder how this is possible? *Welcome home.* The dolphin is speaking to me as it bobs upright, it's curved snout forming a friendly smile. I am delighted…until I wake up.

After I got up, I noticed that Lulu's realtor friend, Tania Horowitz, wasted no time in getting the house listed. A big For Sale sign sat on the front yard with Tania's smiling image.

The interior decorators had descended on the property and efficiently staged the entire house within five days. Lulu's home looked like a highly stylized spread from Architectural Digest.

All her homey furniture had been replaced by high end replicas. Lulu's funky comfortable sofa was replaced by a bold, cream-colored sectional with an oval glass and chrome coffee table in front of a geometric patterned kilim wool rug.

Everything extraneous such as her soft, square, leather poufs was removed, and though the living room was more spacious and brighter, it felt a little sterile. Behind the sofa were six framed, abstract prints. As we toured her home after the stagers left, Lulu stared in shock at how different her home looked.

"I'm afraid to sit down," she sighed.

"Do you like it?"

She shrugged. "It's just so different than what I expected."

"What'd they do with your old furniture?"

"It's in their warehouse." She flopped down on the mega sofa. "This is so surreal."

"It looks nice."

Lulu looked sad. "I can't believe I'm doing this. It's been my home for twenty years."

Part of me wanted to beg her to not sell. Lulu had been so kind to me, even waiving the security deposit when I signed the lease. I knew she'd be happier with her daughter and granddaughter in Hawaii. At seventy-five, who knew how much longer she'd be around to enjoy them?

I sat down next to her and patted her hand. "You always said you'd go back to the islands."

"You'll visit won't you? I'll be upset if you don't!"

"I dreamt about the islands last night. I was swimming with a dolphin. It was so cool."

The sensation of being weightless in the water and diving carelessly came back to me. It was an oddly comforting feeling.

"Your girlfriend Kai once said you were part fish. She said when you were kids, you two would spend hours at the neighborhood pool."

Fond memories of Kai and I splashing in the lap pool made me smile. We took turns holding our breath underwater to see who would last the longest. I always won.

"When did you meet Kai?"

"Last year, when she came out with her wife. Remember…we all met for dinner."

"I do remember—it seems so long ago. I wish you weren't moving. It won't be the same without you, Lulu."

She gave me a playful shove. "Look at you… you have men coming out of the woodwork. You won't even notice I'm gone."

I sighed. *"I will notice.* I don't know what I'm doing dating two men. Some nights I lay awake and think about running away and starting fresh."

How freeing it would be to start over where no one knew you. You could make up your own stories and not be burdened by others' opinions. Lulu reached over and patted my hand fondly. "You've been through a lot. Enjoy the attention. I had a good feeling about you when we first met. I wish there was family to look after *you.*"

"I'm fine. I've been on my own for a long time. I've got great friends."

"I'm sure your mother regretted abandoning you," Lulu said earnestly. "But she had her hands full with a sickly baby boy."

I knew Lulu meant well, but my face flushed with discomfort. I didn't like people feeling sorry for me, and I rarely talked about my past. I'd chosen to forget the crushing disappointment I'd felt throughout my childhood when my mother said she'd come for me. Now, Lulu's soft gaze made something crumble inside me, and hot tears trickled down my face as I realized I wished I'd had a loving mother like her. Someone who rooted for me and cared.

"My ex-husband's been texting me. He wants to take me to dinner. He promised he had a check for me."

Lulu rolled her eyes. "You're not actually going, are you?"

I shook my head and shrugged. "I don't know."

"If he was an honorable man, he would have paid you back by now. I'm glad you left him."

"He didn't give me a choice. He up and left one day after one of his drinking binges and ghosted me. I had no idea where he'd gone or if he was alright."

"That's horrible. Yes, you did have a choice… you could have stuck it out. I know lots of women who would have stayed because they're too scared to be alone."

"My bestie Kai wouldn't have let me. She was livid when she found out and made me go see a divorce attorney."

I grimly recalled the initial consultation with the attorney. She was young and fresh-faced and quietly listened to my story of abandonment. She had advised me to change the locks on the front door, change my email, and block Jason on my cell phone. As I listened to her legal advice, there was a stubborn voice in my head that insisted Jason would come back and make things right. When she noticed my lack of response, she told me to think it over. I'd left the law office in a trance. Could my twenty-year marriage really end ignominiously like this?

Lulu patted my hand affectionately. "You have good friends. Promise me you won't meet him. Tell him to send it to your divorce attorney's office."

"You're right. I'm going to text him now." I got up and went back to my place, where I sat down on the wrought iron garden bench outside. I felt like a deflated balloon as a wave of fatigue swept over me. Part of me didn't care about the money anymore—I just wanted to be done with Jason. My phone buzzed, and I saw that it was my bestie, Kai, calling from Hawaii.

"Aloha!" Her voice sounded muffled, and I could tell she was calling from her car.

"Aloha. I hope you're using your Bluetooth."

"Of course. I was just thinking of you. When're you coming for a visit?"

"It might be sooner than later. My landlady just put her house up for sale. So I might be homeless."

"Well, you definitely need to come stay with Shara and me. We've got plenty of space, plus, we have that Airstream in back. You're welcome to crash there."

"I thought you were renting it out."

"Yes, to Diana while she was overseeing the remodel. But she's gone."

"Could I bring Rodrigo?"

"Bring whoever you want."

The sound of her happy, lilting voice cheered me. I thought about her modest off-grid hobby farm and yoga retreat near Hilo on the Big Island. *Some nights I lay awake and think about running away and starting fresh.* My own words from earlier echoed in my mind.

"You won't believe who showed up at my front door the other day."

"Jason."

"Bingo.

"Did he have a briefcase of cash?"

"If only."

"What'd he want?"

I filled her in and included the part of Rodrigo calling Jason out.

"Good for him. Rodrigo sounds like a cool guy. So, what do you think? You're not doing anything… so come on out. We can catch up, and you can bring me some goodies from Trader Joes!"

"Let me guess. The Joe Joe cookies, peanut butter caramel popcorn and sea salt brownie bites."

She chuckled. "You got it, sister."

Kai had a voracious sweet tooth and one of those enviable, petite bodies with a mega metabolism. I'd seen her enthusiastically pack away double cheeseburgers with a large order of fries, topped off with a chocolate milkshake with whipped cream. She never gained an ounce. Whereas I looked at a pastry and could feel my butt expanding.

I sent Jason a terse message to contact my attorney, then thought about the Pescion Café and how the staff there were like family. Especially Blake James, his restaurant manager. One day, feeling depressed and worn down, I'd decided to go for a swim at the gym. After I parked my car, I had been surprised to bump into Jason's former restaurant manager, Blake James. He'd parked next to me and tapped on my car window, startling me. I rolled down the window.

"Hey, girlfriend."

"Hey, yourself." I got out of the car and we hugged.

"How are you doing?"

I saw his expression, and I knew he *knew*. "So, you heard?"

He nodded in sympathy and put a comforting arm around my shoulders. "You know I love you guys, but Jason's being a dick."

"I saw a divorce attorney the other day."

"Let's grab some coffee and talk."

He took my hand, and we went to Peet's nearby, where he got me a latte and we sat outside at a small, wrought iron garden table. The mall was bustling with shoppers, and I had that disquieting feeling of being out of sync. Smiling, chatty people strolled past us purposefully with shopping bags, while I sat contemplating the end of my marriage.

"Babe, I owe Jason a lot. He took a chance and promoted me from a server to a restaurant manager. I'll always remember how he believed in me. But… I have no illusions that he can be a narcissistic dick. Just taking off like that—not *cool*. You deserve better."

"I knew things were bad. We hadn't had sex in over a year. Some nights he'd come home and just crash on the sofa. I knew we were drifting apart. I just didn't want to admit it."

"Well, shit… you guys have been together like fifteen years?"

"Twenty. But who's counting?"

"Man, when my parents split, I was ecstatic. They'd been miserable for years. I actually wanted to throw a party!"

Blake looked impeccable as always, wearing a black and gray striped t-shirt over light gray cargo sweatpants and white running shoes. The outfit showcased his lean, tight physique. His attire was topped off by black Ray-Ban sunglasses.

"Do you know that guy?"

Blake lifted his paper coffee cup and gestured at someone ordering coffee inside. I turned and saw my physical therapist, Rodrigo. It looked like he was on his way to work because instead of his customary light blue scrubs, he had on a black Giants t-shirt over blue jeans and black Birkenstock sandals.

"That's Rodrigo. He's the physical therapist who was treating my frozen shoulder."

"He's been staring at you since we sat down."

Before I could respond, Rodrigo came over to say hello.

"Fancy meeting you here!" he joked.

"Hi. You headed to work?" I asked.

He nodded and took a sip of his coffee. "I hope I'm not interrupting anything."

"This is my friend Blake. He used to work for my husband."

"Soon to be *ex-husband*," Blake quipped.

"I'm sorry to hear that," Rodrigo said.

"It's for the best," Blake said.

My face flushed. "It's a long story."

"If you'd like to talk… or if there's anything you need," Rodrigo said. He reached into his jeans pocket and pulled out a worn, black, leather wallet, extracting a business card. "That's my cell phone on the back."

"That's sweet of you."

"She might need help moving." Blake winked at me, and I blushed again.

"Sure, I'd be happy to help. Sorry—I've gotta run."

He nodded at Blake. As Blake watched Rodrigo amble away, he lowered his sunglasses and made lip smacking noises.

"He's got a nice ass."

"He's *nice…* in general."

"See… the universe is already telling you to move on by sending you a yummy hot dude."

"You weren't exactly subtle."

"My mother used to tell me that the quickest way to get over a man… is to get under another man!"

"Did you always follow your mother's advice?"

He winked at me. "*Always!*"

One month later, I would bump into Rodrigo at the salad bar.

***

My phone suddenly chirped, and I looked down to see Jason's response.

"*Whatever.*"

Asshole.

Chapter Seven

I could hardly keep up with Cassie as she power-walked ahead of me on the paved bike path. She was dressed in her usual Lululemon workout outfit—an oversized teal blue hoodie over matching sweatpants and black walking shoes.

I breathlessly trudged behind her as she chugged ahead, passing dog walkers, mothers with strollers, and joggers. She looked back at me and laughed.

"You better up your cardio routine, girlfriend!"

"I know," I panted.

"Sex doesn't count, either!"

I was glad I'd left my gray hoodie back in Cassie's SUV—I was sweating profusely. I'd put on a black crop top over gray leggings and wore my black Keene walking shoes. But even with the cooling ocean breeze coming over the San Francisco Bay, I felt no relief. I was having the mother-of-all hot flashes. I needed to get my hormone cream dosage checked. I was also too scared to get on the bathroom scale because I noticed my leggings were extra snug around my stomach. Ugh.

"I need to take a break," I said.

Cassie jogged in place as I went over to a wooden bench, rested my outstretched leg on top, and bent over, hoping to loosen my hamstrings. I tried not to think about the twenty pounds I'd put on, lost, and put on again after Covid.

I could feel Cassie getting impatient as she jogged in place, and I knew she had a busy day ahead before she picked up her daughter from school. She'd recited her dizzying list of errands in the car on the way over.

"Go on… I'll catch up with you on the way back," I said finally.

She nodded briefly and jogged off. I did some more stretching and plopped down with relief on the wooden bench, closing my eyes and breathing deeply as I took in the salty sea air, the cool breeze, and sunlight on my face. When I opened my eyes again, I saw a black crow hopping on the grass across from me. He stopped and stared at me, so I stood up and walked over to him and he remained perfectly still, looking up at me with a steady gaze. Then I heard Cassie behind me.

"Hey…we've got to get going. You still feel like Peet's coffee?"

Cassie appeared before me, her face flushed and sweaty. She still looked perfect sans make-up, with rosy cheeks and blemish-free porcelain skin.

"Did you see that crow?"

"What crow? You were by yourself."

"*Up there!*"

She shaded her eyes with her hand and squinted.

"Nope. "

She started swinging her arms around in big circles, then proceeded to do side lunges. I started to disagree but let it drop.

"Kai just posted herself on Instagram wearing her prom dress. I can't believe she's still like a size two!" Cassie said.

"High school seems like a hundred years ago. Little did I know how much simpler my life was back then. Life wasn't perfect, but we had dreams and optimism."

I had so desperately wanted to get married to Declan and start a family. I'd fantasized about our cute house and the white picket fence. Cassie stopped stretching and nodded behind me. "Is that Jason and Candace?"

I looked down the bike trail and was surprised to see my ex-husband with his former business partner. They walked close together, their heads bowed down in an intimate conversation. Candace was wearing a snug, red and purple sports bra over black, high-cut shorts and black running shoes. Her augmented breasts were spilling over the bra top, and I could make out the curve of her sizeable implants. A red headband covered most of her forehead, and her blonde hair stuck out in straw-colored tufts. Jason surprisingly had on the same outfit I'd last seen him in, the black and white silk shirt, black leather jacket, and jeans. He tended to be minimalist, so I wasn't surprised.

"What do you want to do?" Cassie asked.

"We should act normal and say hello."

They were so engrossed in their conversation, they almost ran into us. Jason noticed us first and seemed surprised. Candace shifted uneasily on her feet, not looking at me. She seemed like she was trying to gauge the emotional temperature between Jason and me.

"Hey. Fancy meeting you two here," he said. He nodded at Cassie.

"We were just getting caught up," Candace blurted. "We're brainstorming on another restaurant."

"*Here?*" I asked.

Candace looked at Jason. "We're just in the beginning stages. Nothing concrete. But, yeah… somewhere close by." She put her hand on Jason's shoulder as if for confirmation. I was surprised by how intensely jealous I felt seeing the two of them together. Something twisted in my stomach, and my jaw tightened.

"I didn't hear back from you about dinner," Jason said to me. Candace's eyes widened slightly but she quickly looked away.

"How about tonight?" I said.

"I'm good with tonight."

"Our usual spot?"

Jason smiled smugly. "*Absolutely.*"

As they moved past us, Jason nodded at Cassie.

She put her hand on my arm. "What *are* you doing?"

"I don't know."

"Take it from me, you don't what to go *there*," Cassie warned.

I didn't respond, and Cassie sighed in resignation. "Just be careful, okay?"

***

Lulu was making banana bread when I got home from my walk with Cassie. Her formerly spikey white hair was now rose pink. She had on a long, cotton, pink muumuu dress with white hibiscus flowers, padding around in her black, rubber flip-flop sandals.

"So… when you going back to Hawaii?" she asked.

Lulu took out two loaves of banana bread and rested them on a dish towel on the kitchen counter. She had also made a pot of jasmine green tea, and the pleasing floral scent perfumed the kitchen. I sat down at her round, walnut dining table as she poured the tea into glass mugs.

"I'm still thinking about it."

"What's there to think about?" Lulu looked genuinely surprised.

"I don't have the best memories. I was born there but left when I was five. Then I didn't return for thirty years when Jason and I honeymooned there."

I tried to think about how to explain my on-going ennui about the islands. My honeymoon had been romantic and epic, with moonlight beach walks and swimming with dolphins. The honeymoon had been followed by Jason's six-month restaurant contract at a popular local restaurant. But then that was when his drinking escalated. The last time I'd returned was for my brother's funeral. Not great memories.

"Didn't you go to a wedding on the Big Island?" Lulu asked.

"Yes, I went to my bestie Kai's wedding. Kai and I have been best friends since high school."

I fished my phone from my purse and pulled up an old high school picture of us. "This is from our prom."

Lulu put on her reading glasses and peered over my shoulder. "Look how cute you girls are."

I studied the picture fondly. Kai had worn an Esprit, purple-sequined, flowered mini dress with black, leather, platform sandals. Her thick, black hair flowed in waves over her shoulders. In contrast, I'd worn a pale-pink and white, lace, Gunne Sax dress with sandals. My hair was pulled back in a loose topknot, with sprigs of Baby's Breath flowers tucked behind my right ear.

"Look at those platform shoes. How did she walk around in those things? My feet ache just looking at the picture!" Lulu said.

"I used to walk all over San Francisco wearing those. I don't know how I did it without killing myself," I said.

Lulu scrolled through some more of my prom pictures. "Who's that handsome man?"

"That was my prom date, Declan Murphy. We dated during my senior year."

"He looks like Prince Harry with that gorgeous red hair."

I squinted at Declan's picture. The only resemblance I could see besides the ginger hair was freckles. Prince Harry had blue eyes and Declan had brown eyes and higher cheekbones.

"I lost my virginity to him in the back of his father's silver-blue Mercedes on prom night. We ditched the prom early and drove to the beach instead."

"You naughty girl." Lulu chuckled.

I remembered how clever Declan and I thought we were, sneaking out past the adult chaperones. We ended up at Ocean Beach getting drunk on Tattinger champagne he took from his father's wine collection, sipping the bubbly from paper cups, and I had liked the way it made me feel instantly giddy. We'd sat on the chilly, damp sand, tacitly listening to the roar of the surf as we huddled under a scratchy, old, Army wool blanket.

"Are you nervous about tonight?" Lulu asked.

"A little."

"I think it's great you're going to finally confront Jason. Clear the air. This ghosting crap is *bullshit*. You've got this."

"Thanks for the vote of confidence."

Lulu suddenly got up from the table. "I almost forgot. This came in today for you."

She handed me a FedEx envelope, and I tore it open, finding a plain white envelope with my name written on it in Jason's writing. The envelope was unsealed, and a check for fifty thousand dollars was inside. It was going to be an interesting night.

Chapter Eight

We met at the Waterbar Restaurant along the San Francisco waterfront. The restaurant was right underneath the Bay Bridge, which was lit up brightly with Christmas-tree-like shimmering lights. We had met here for the first time twenty-one years earlier.

I decided to take the ferry over across the Bay. I was too nervous to drive, and I never navigated downtown city traffic very well. As I walked from the ferry building down the wharf toward the restaurant, I saw Jason leaning against the concrete railing.

He was dressed smartly in a tailored gray suit with a light-gray polo shirt underneath the jacket. As I got closer, my heart fluttered rapidly with that same visceral, magnetic pull from years ago. It was a magical scene, with the glowing bay bridge set against a silvery swirl of fog. A faint, luminous silhouette of a pearl-white full moon hung overhead in the sky. He turned toward me when I was several feet away, and our eyes met.

"You look amazing," he said.

"You look nice too."

I was glad I took the time to dress up. I'd gone for the classic little black dress, a sleeveless wool shift with my pink shawl, black leather ankle boots, and simple pearl jewelry.

"I'm glad you decided to come."

"Thank you for sending the money."

"I'm sorry it took so long."

As we neared the restaurant, I thought about all the celebrations we'd shared here—birthdays and anniversaries, among other moments. As we entered the restaurant, I was glad to see it hadn't changed. The cavernous space was decorated in rustic, dark-wood accents that gave it a cozy ambience. The centerpiece of the dining room were two huge, glass, cylindrical fish tanks, complete with undulating seaweed and tropical fish.

The restaurant was buzzing with activity, and I was overwhelmed from din of loud conversations and the crowd. Sensing my discomfort, Jason took me gently by the elbow.

"Let's sit outside," he said.

It was calmer on the stone patio. There were large, canvas, patio umbrellas mixed with heat lamps near each table. Jason rested his hands on the dining table.

"Something wrong?" I asked.

He shook his head. "I wasn't sure you'd come."

"I had second thoughts. And third thoughts," I admitted.

"I know I screwed up this past year."

I didn't know how to respond. Thankfully, our server arrived and took our drink orders. I ordered a glass of Chardonnay, and Jason ordered a beer.

"We both made a lot of mistakes," I said. "I don't think it's helpful to rehash the past. We just have to move on."

"What does that even look like? I wish we could go back to the way it was. The good times."

His sentiment surprised me.

"I don't think that's possible."

"We could try."

I sat in disbelief. I'd fantasized about this moment intermittently for months. In my fantasies, he was pathetically contrite. He'd cry and get on his knees to beg for forgiveness, and I'd blow him off. I'd tell him I had a younger, hot lover and watch him suffer. But now that it was actually happening, I didn't know how to react.

"I can't go back to the way it was. All you ever cared about was the restaurant."

"That's not true."

I threw my hands up in frustration. "We're already arguing over the same things!"

I noticed people around us staring because of our raised voices. It'd been a mistake to come. Nothing had changed. The server returned with our drinks and discreetly placed them in front of us, then left quickly. I took a sip of my wine, while Jason stared at his beer silently. He got up abruptly and threw down cash on the table.

"This was a bad idea. I thought we could talk this out, but I guess I was wrong."

I watched him storm off, deflated and embarrassed. I thought about texting Cassie or Kai but decided against it, took another sip of wine, and got up. If I hurried, I could catch the last ferry back. I started walking down the waterfront back to the ferry terminal. As I got close to the ticket booth, I heard Jason's voice behind me.

"Come back with me to the hotel. Let's just talk. You want to move forward, so let's do this."

I should have said no.

***

What am I doing? We silently rode back to the Stanford Court Hotel in a taxi. He put his hand over mine in the back seat, and an electric jolt shot through me.

We entered the deserted hotel lobby without speaking and rode up the elevator. The room was a spacious suite with a king bed and a nice view of the Transamerica Pyramid building. The once controversial white, obelisk building was silhouetted against the inky night sky like an otherworldly edifice in a science fiction movie. A dense swirl of silvery fog obscured the forty-eight-story building except for the peaked top. It was hard to see anything through the thick, misty fog, and an unsettling sensation fluttered in my stomach. Jason came up behind me and put his arms around my waist, then leaned over and nuzzled my neck. I melted into him—the familiarity of his presence and the scent of his musky aftershave made me unravel.

I turned around and he kissed me forcefully. As his tongue met mine, it felt like an elixir flooded my entire being. We fell on the bed and our clothes came off quickly, landing in a messy heap on the floor.

The sexy feeling of his bare skin against mine ignited something inside me. My body bloomed as he caressed me in the usual intimate places, and I eagerly opened my legs to receive him. It was comforting and soothing to feel him inside me again. He climaxed noisily within minutes and rolled off me with a sigh. The brief but passionate lovemaking made me want him even more. I climbed on top of him and kissed him deeply as I slowly rubbed myself against him.

"*Jesus!*" he moaned.

In moments, he was ready to go again, and I straddled him, feeling him snugly inside. Jason sat up as I wrapped my legs around his waist. He buried his face between my breasts, and I felt an instant *zing* as he suckled a nipple. It was enough to put me over the edge, and a liquid warmth fanned out between my legs. We clung to each other, sweating and panting heavily.

"I need some water," he said.

We disentangled our limbs, and I slid off, the cool, crisp sheets soothing as I pulled them over myself. Jason went to the mini fridge and pulled out bottled water and two glasses. He took a thirsty swig from the bottle and then filled the glasses, returning to hand me one as he perched on the edge of the bed.

"We still got it, baby," Jason said.

"We've *always* had it."

He gently pushed a tendril of hair off my face and tucked it behind my ear. "You hungry?"

"Starved."

"How about some Super Duper burgers? One mini burger, one bird sando, and one super burger."

"Extra mayo, garlic fries, and chocolate milk shake!" I added.

He retrieved his iPhone and punched up his Door Dash app, then got back into bed with me, and I snuggled against him. He kissed the top of my head.

"Were you expecting *this*?" he asked.

"Not in a million years. Were *you*?"

"Let's just say I'm more than pleasantly surprised."

"So, what did you do with yourself the past year… besides ghosting me?"

"I'm sorry. I know I was a total jerk. I went back to Seattle for a while and hung out with my daughter. I picked up some consulting gigs, and I thought about you constantly—about how to make things right."

"So, what's this new project Candace mentioned earlier?"

"We're looking at opening a wine bar in Sausalito."

"So, you two didn't hook up this past year?"

"Of course not. We're strictly business partners. I've always said that. Why don't you believe me?"

He seemed sincere, but a wariness stopped me from completely believing him. I changed the subject, not wanting to dwell on the two of them together.

"I'm headed to Oahu next week to see Kai."

"How's she doing? She and Shara still together?"

"Still together and going strong. She got certified as a yoga instructor *and* got her massage therapist license."

"Good for her. She was always such a go-getter."

There was a knock at the door and the sound of shuffling feet outside in the hallway.

"That was fast," I said.

Jason got up and opened the door to retrieve our dinner. The oily smell of garlic fries made me instantly ravenous. I was startled to see a six pack of Stella Artois beer.

"*Beer?* I didn't know Door Dash delivered booze."

"Sure, why not? I'm legal," he joked.

"But… I thought you were on the wagon."

"*Relax*. I'm not drinking it all tonight."

I was disappointed at his casual dismissal and wondered if he was still going to AA meetings. A jab of uneasiness rippled over me. Jason laid out a white bath towel on the bed and arranged our food on top.

"Look, if me drinking a beer is going to upset you, I won't.

"I'd rather you didn't.

He shrugged. "No problem."

He got up and put the beer away. I was relieved. I didn't know why food tasted so good after sex, but everything was sublime. I was embarrassed at how quickly I'd consumed my sandwich and fries, slurping the last of the chocolate shake noisily as Jason looked on in bemusement. He had barely finished his burger.

"I've missed *this*."

I raised my eyebrows in askance.

"Watching you chow down and enjoying every bite. How you ate like a famished linebacker on our first date—buffalo wings, French dip sandwich, fries, a root beer float, and half my apple pie!"

I grimaced.

"Those days are over. I'm low carb and intermittent fasting just for maintenance!"

"You still look amazing."

"Flattery will get you everywhere." I crumbled up all the paper food wrappers and the paper milkshake cup and put them in the garbage can by the nearby desk.

"What do *you* miss about us?"

I found my underpants near the footboard of the bed and slipped them back on, then stretched out on the bed. "I miss sleeping in on Sundays and going shopping at the farmers market. I miss having Nutella crepes and cappuccinos for breakfast after we went shopping."

He bowed his head in contemplation. "No one ever figured I'd settle down… until I met you."

He finished his burger, got up, and tossed the rest of the paper wrappers, stepping into the marble-tiled bathroom to wash his hands. He forked his fingers through his hair, smoothing down his mussed-up tresses, came back to bed, and slid in close to me, spoon-style like we used to. It felt familiar and soothing, but a niggling feeling jabbed at me. We still had chemistry, but after the past year, I knew that wasn't enough. I was having stellar sex with Rodrigo, and I trusted him more than the man I'd spent twenty years with. Instead of feeling a cozy post-coital afterglow, I felt empty. My desire to have Jason back the way we were was unrealistic. We'd both changed so much.

Jason ran his fingers down my arm in a caress.

"What's going to happen now?"

"Right this second or in the big picture?"

"Either… or?"

I shrugged. "Let's take it one day at a time."

He leaned over and kissed me. "Sounds good."

I remembered Cassie's warning and wondered if I'd made a huge mistake.

***

I woke up to the sound of the shower water running in the bathroom and squinted at the clock radio next to the bed. It was still early. I yawned and sat up, noting my panties were back on the floor. After dinner, we'd had another robust lovemaking session and eventually drifted off to sleep. I was hungry for breakfast and wondered if I should go get coffee while he was in the shower.

I heard his iPhone ping and looked over to see a text from Candace. It started with: *"Hey, lover boy. Missed you last night."*

I knew I had no right to snoop, but I clicked on the message.

"Thought you were coming by after dinner with Noel. Guess things got interesting. Here's a hint of what you missed."

There was a graphic photo of her overtly augmented bare breasts. A silver nipple ring pierced the right pink aureole. My face flushed with anger. *Strictly business my ass.* My heart pounded so loudly I thought it would explode out of my chest. I threw on my clothes, grabbed my shoes and purse, and raced out of the hotel room. I couldn't deal with the overwhelming tide of rage that swept over me. I had to get away.

Chapter Nine

I sat by myself at the noisy gate at San Francisco International airport, waiting for the pre-boarding announcement. I was an emotional wreck. Not only did I have sex with my ex-husband, I know I hurt Rodrigo with my abrupt decision to leave for Hawaii.

For the past several days, Rodrigo and I exchanged texts and voice messages. He wanted to come by before I left for the islands, but I couldn't bear to see him. He didn't ask what happened when I was with Jason, but I think he *knew*.

His text read, "I don't judge what you may have done with him." Then he texted me a video clip of the Don Henley song "The Last Worthless Evening" the night before. He quoted a lyric about trusting in love again that made me break down in tears. I sobbed for an hour, feeling sorry for myself and how weak I was.

I *knew* being with Jason was a mistake. *What was wrong with me?*

In between Rodrigo's messages, I had to field several voicemails and texts from Jason. He wanted to explain about Candace's sext message. They weren't hooking up. He swore on his mother's grave that it was Candace's poor, drunken judgment. I didn't know what to think.

I had slept poorly the night before, and the tedious TSA line at the airport gate hadn't helped my depleted emotional disposition. The only comfort I got was several texts from Kai and Cassie, reassuring me that I'd done nothing wrong. Thank God for them.

To pass the time, I had written in my butterfly diary and jotted down a dream I'd had the night before. I was at Jason's restaurant, and when I looked out the window, I saw an Orca whale near the boat ramp. Candace stood next to me and told me it was a fake whale. "It's plastic—someone put there as a prank." She laughed at me.

Great. Now Candace was haunting my unconscious mind.

I was relieved when I heard the boarding announcement. Pretty soon, I'd be with Kai and far away from my crazy soap opera life.

***

When I awoke on the plane, my mouth was dry and my eyes were itchy. I'd managed to doze off for a while and was relieved when the pilot announced the final descent to the Daniel K. Inouye airport in Honolulu was imminent. Despite watching an action adventure movie and reading a murder mystery book on Kindle, the five-hour flight seemed to drag on

Across the aisle, an elderly couple named Stan and Gloria were celebrating their fiftieth anniversary. They were dressed in matching Hawaiian outfits. The husband's aloha shirt was mint green with colorful Hibiscus flowers in orange and purple. The wife had on a matching design in a long, flowing muumuu dress with puffy cap sleeves.

It struck me how long-time married couples started to resemble each other in curious ways. They both had downy, white hair like Norfin troll dolls and long, deeply-etched faces. Earlier, there had been an in-flight announcement shortly after takeoff that Stan and Gloria had honeymooned in Hawaii back in 1974. Everyone enthusiastically applauded, and they got complimentary rum drinks. Gloria's pale, thin face was flushed from alcohol and excitement.

She leaned over toward me. "Are you going home, dear?" she asked.

"I was born on the islands. But San Francisco's my home."

She patted my hand. "How nice. We have such beautiful memories of our wedding on the beach. *Fifty years* ago!"

Her husband Stan leaned over and pecked her on the cheek fondly. "Fifty wonderful years. Three beautiful children. God's been good to us!"

"We've been blessed." Gloria sighed.

Stan agreed and sipped his rum drunk and closed his eyes. Their loving exchange made me envious. I'd barely made it to twenty years. There wouldn't be any golden years for me with a devoted husband. I pushed away the bitter thoughts.

My immediate seatmates to my left were an attractive young Indian couple in their mid-twenties. Just after takeoff from SFO, they had both pulled out their laptops and proceeded to studiously peruse their work emails. The husband wore a blue collared polo shirt that had a Silicon Valley logo on it. It felt strange to be sitting next to someone without being acknowledged. They had gotten up to use the bathroom once and nodded politely as I got up to let them pass. Definitely one of the perks of booking ahead was reserving an aisle seat.

Since we were moments away from landing, I leaned over to address the young woman next to me. "First time to Hawaii?" I asked.

She looked up from her laptop. "No. We usually go to Maui but thought we'd try something different and check out the North Shore. It's our *honeymoon.*"

She had a pretty smile. Her husband glanced over and smiled in acknowledgement at me.

"We actually got married in Big Sur last month and had brief honeymoon there," he added.

They had that incandescent new love glow. A jab of pain pierced my chest. *That was me twenty years ago. Jason and I had held hands during the flight and sipped champagne in first class.*

The wife gestured to Stan and Gloria. "So romantic. Will that be us, sweetheart?" She gave her husband a teasing smile. He reached over and put his hand over hers.

I noticed her sparkling platinum, diamond wedding set. It was easily worth thirty thousand dollars—I had looked at a similar setting when I got engaged at the famous Shreve jewelry store in Union Square. My own modest wedding set was sitting in a safe deposit box at the bank. Another post-divorce loose end that I didn't know how to handle.

The pilot announced the final descent, and we all dutifully put up our food trays and buckled up.

***

Airports were stressful for me. I didn't like the sensory overload of so much busyness as throngs of people hurried around me. I caught snippets of loud and inane cell phone conversations as well as crying babies. The constant noise of airline announcements over the public address system added to hectic background noise. *Where is Kai?* Kai's time management was always a bit off, and it irritated me when I counted on her to show up on time. Then I heard a familiar voice behind me.

"Aloha, *Minnow!*"

Kai was quite a sight with her off-shoulder, bright-green and pale-blue muumuu dress and a ti leaf *haku* crown. A waft of plumeria perfume floated off her tan skin.

"You haven't called me that in years*!*" I said as we hugged.

"I know right… it popped into my head just now. Hey, sorry I'm late. Traffic backed up on H1. How was the flight?"

"Good."

A loud buzzing noise sounded as the luggage carousel started to churn in a slow circle. Several black, gray, and blue suitcases tumbled down the chute and onto the carousel. I was surprised to see my pink overnight suitcase eject out of the chute and shouldered my way through dense crowd hovering around the carousel.

"That is one pink suitcase. It's like a bubblegum pink!" Kai said.

"Lulu gifted it to me. She had an extra one and insisted I take it."

"Well, you can't miss that one."

I saw the Indian couple nearby, holding hands and sweetly kissing. I pointed them out to Kai.

"*Honeymooners,*" I said.

"They're cute. You'll find someone again, *I know it.* "

"Are you being nice, or did you have a vision?"

"Both."

"Have I met this person yet?"

"*Maybe.*" She winked at me. "Things are still unfolding. Timelines are shifting."

We'd been besties since high school, and yet Kai's spontaneous and unerringly accurate prognostications still surprised me. She had even predicted me meeting Jason years ago.

As I thought about that, I asked, "Did you know Jason and I were going to split up?"

"No. The ancestors don't tell me everything."

"What have they been telling you lately?"

"That you need to be here and soak up the vibes. And no, I'm not being nice… that was a direct message, and you aren't getting back with Jason."

Of course, I knew that. Still, hearing Kai stating it so bluntly hurt. We started walking toward the parking garage.

"How's Rodrigo? You miss him already?"

"Yes. I didn't leave things on a good note."

I thought about the Don Henley song and my throat closed up. Kai was bouncing along next to me, looking at her iPhone.

"I feel like I messed up things with Rodrigo."

"You worry too much. He's a big boy."

We headed out of the airport and crossed the street to the parking garage, immediately shrouded by warm, humid air. Kai's Ford Ranger truck was close by, and we left the airport, heading on the H1 freeway toward East Oahu.

Kai's in-laws owned an Airbnb rental in the Hawaii Kai subdivision. As we drove down the Kalaniana'ole Highway past pristine beach parks and strip malls, I felt strangely content. Kai was playing Iz Kamakawiwo'ole singing "Somewhere Over the Rainbow," which was my theme song whenever I came to visit. His soulful voice always stayed with me when I went back to California.

"What's on your mind?" Kai asked.

"Food!"

"There's some peanuts and dried fruit to tide you over in the glove compartment."

I leaned over and opened the glove compartment to find a sealed plastic bag of roasted peanuts. There was also a bag of dried apricots.

"There's a new place at Koko Marina that serves really good *loco moco*. We'll go there," Kai added.

Within minutes, we pulled into the Koko Marina shopping center. I fondly recalled meals at Zippy's diner nearby and was curious about the new place. Kai parked near Ted's Burgers, and we got out.

The Heavenly Island restaurant was decorated in a fun, boho style, with soothing shades of beige, gray-blue, and white. Overstuffed chairs faced the azure-blue waters of the boat marina, and after we were seated, Kai ordered us tropical ice teas right away.

"I'm so glad you're here. It feels like forever since we hung out together."

"It was last year when you and Shara came out for her family reunion. I met you for lunch in Napa at the hotel. Cassie and I were just talking about the fact that the three of us haven't been together for ten years."

"*Really?* Since the wedding?"

"You were supposed to come out and meet us in the wine country, but something happened."

Kai rolled her eyes. "Oh yeah. Shara's mother fell and broke her hip, so I had to stay behind to take care of the animals. But I thought we all met up in Carmel later that year?"

"It was just me. Cassie's daughter got the flu, so she stayed at home. Do you miss California?"

"Not really. I never felt like I belonged. It started in high school when people made fun of my name."

I raised my eyebrows. "You're kidding, right? You were the most popular girl in high school. I was the one who didn't fit in."

"I'm not kidding. You and Declan were so popular and cute together. Remember the prom... Cassie and I went together because we couldn't get dates."

"You wore that purple Esprit dress."

Ahe grinned and nodded. "You wore a lace Gunne Sax dress. Declan wore a gray tuxedo, and he picked you up in his father's Benz."

"Wow... that seems so long ago."

"So... who's this new guy Cassie's involved with?"

"His name's Montrell. He's her personal trainer, and he's thirty."

"He looks so young on her Instagram pictures—like he just graduated from high school. Leave it to Cassie to seduce her personal trainer."

"I think it was the other way around."

We studied the menu, and Kai put hers down. "I'm going to have pancakes. You?"

"I always have to have loco moco."

"Before I forget, check this out." She fished out her iPhone from her purse and thumbed through the screen. With a smile, she showed me a photo of a handsome surfer.

"Guess who that is?"

I shook my head. "I have no clue."

"That's my cousin Lono."

"*What?*"

I squinted at the photo again, trying to reconcile the scrawny boy I remembered with the robust, physically perfect male specimen on Kai's phone.

"Wow, he sure grew up."

"No kidding. He's teaching me how to speak Hawaiian."

"You really are going native."

"We should start using our real names from now on."

"We do use our real names."

"I mean, you should go by *Noelani* instead of Noel. I've already changed my name back to Kailani. It was different when we were in school in California. We were trying to fit in—two brown girls with no parents in a white-bread town. Remember when I begged my *Tutu* to change my name to

Karen. Can you believe that? Lono's inspired me to embrace our heritage."

"I'm not Hawaiian. You are… both your parents are from here."

"You were born here too."

"But… my mother was born in San Francisco like Aunt Lily. She was Chinese, and I have no idea what my father was. Now I don't even have any family left."

Kai put her hand over mine. "Yes you do. *I'm your family.* We'll always be sisters."

My eyes pricked with tears. Kailani descended from three generations of native Hawaiians. Throughout our long friendship, I had envied her lineage and her big, noisy, loving family. Even though she was an only child, she had lots of aunts, uncles, and cousins. I barely knew my biological mother. My Aunt Lily rarely talked about her or my grandparents. She knew nothing about my biological father. He wasn't even listed on my birth certificate.

"How is your grandmother doing?" I asked.

"She's fine. She asked about you."

I smiled and sighed, "Your family's always been so nice to me. I still can't believe that Lono, that skinny kid who came to visit during school break, is all grown up."

"And he'll be happy to see you. He ditched his high-stress job in Cali and is hanging out with Shara and me. He's been doing some repairs and gardening on the property. It feels good to have family around."

"I'm still trying to process that the little obnoxious rug rat is a grown man."

She chuckled. "Time goes fast."

***

After lunch, we drove to the house rental that Shara's parents owned. Shara's father was a retired contractor and had added a top floor for visiting family members. We pulled into the driveway and parked.

The two-story house was painted beige, with an oak door. Kailani reached under the doormat, pulled out a house key, and we stepped into the foyer, which smelled of disinfectant. Directly in front of us was a locked oak door. To our right were steep wood stairs that led up to the loft apartment. We went up and stopped at a landing with large windows overlooking the neatly landscaped front garden. The second flight of stairs led to the living room, with a big, comfy-looking, caramel leather sofa. It faced a modest kitchenette with a stove, refrigerator, and farmhouse sink with marble counters. A round, oak, pedestal dining table with four wooden dining chairs sat next to the sofa. Just beyond the kitchen was a small bedroom with a ceiling fan. There was also a window air conditioning unit in the bedroom window, which Kailani turned on.

"Stuffy huh?"

"It's a cute place. Shara's father did all of this by himself?"

"Lono helped." She opened the refrigerator and peered in. "You want a beer? We've got some Sierra Nevada in here."

"You got any diet soda?"

Kailani reached in and pulled out a diet Pepsi for me, helping herself to a bottle of beer. "Come on, let's check out the sitting room."

To the right of the stairs was a TV room with a large, mounted, flatscreen TV and another picture window that overlooked the garden. There was a beige leather loveseat facing the TV with a glass coffee table on the side. Kailani took a healthy swig of beer and flopped down on the loveseat, while I turned on the ceiling fan and sat down next to her.

"Oh, it feels good to chillax. I've got to duck out later to take care of some massage clients. I should have told you—it was a last-minute booking."

"I'll be fine."

"It's a couples' massage in Waikiki. It's good money." She rubbed her thumb, index, and middle fingers together.

"I bet the tips are decent."

"I add twenty percent for the booking. I gotta drive and park downtown—you know how expensive that is."

I wondered what Rodrigo was doing and resisted the urge to text him as Kailani and I sipped our cold drinks quietly. It was nice to finally get here and relax, listening to the *whoosh* of the ceiling fan churning above our heads. I hadn't realized how much I missed her and allowed myself to enjoy the moment.

Chapter Ten

We were having breakfast at Zippy's in the Koko Marina shopping center. I liked the diner feel of the restaurant, with its clean, vinyl upholstered booths and a view of the sparkling marina.

I watched Kailani enviously as she wolfed down her hearty breakfast bento box of steamed white rice, Portuguese sausage, corned beef hash, and scrambled eggs. She was finishing off a side of grilled cornbread as I sipped my coffee, then pushed her plate back with a sigh.

"Girl, you hardly ate anything!" she said. She gestured at my empty plate. I had a cheese omelet minus the steamed rice. She had eaten that too.

"I wish I had your metabolism," I sighed. "You can eat whatever you want."

She shook her head. "*I wish.* I usually skip dinner unless Shara's cooking."

"I miss Jason's cooking. He used to serve me crab eggs benedict in bed."

"No more living in the past, sweetie. You've got a sexy young lover. Focus on *him.*"

"Rodrigo makes this delicious Portuguese breakfast sandwich with linguica sausage, avocado, and salsa."

"*See?* Rodrigo is the anti-Jason… considerate, nurturing, and kind. Not to mention… *easy on the eyes*!"

"Yes, he is," I sighed.

"You've always been the caretaker—you give a hundred and ten percent. You can't help it. But you need a partner that's going to give you back a hundred and ten. That's all I'm saying."

Caretaker? I didn't see myself that way. I just wanted to be a good wife and make my husband happy. I wasn't used to someone taking charge and orchestrating my life. At first, it had been a relief to have someone plan my life out for me. I was content to be a stay-at-home wife, and Jason liked the flexibility it gave us. We took spontaneous weekday trips to the coast or bought last minute concert tickets. I helped him with office work, like printing out new menus, calling guests to confirm dinner party reservations, and helping out with catering orders. We were happy with our arrangement and made a good team.

"Could we drive over to Diamond Head and walk around?" I asked.

"Sure. We can stop and get shaved ice for dessert."

I reached for my wallet, but Kailani waved me off. "You're my guest. Save your money."

She paid the bill, and we slid out of our booth, off to Diamond Head.

***

I smiled at the handsome, bronze-skinned surfer standing in front of me. He was talking to me in pidgin, trying to ask me out.

"Hey, Sista, we go talk story and get some grinds."

In the background, Kailani was practically peeing in her pants, laughing so hard tears were streaming down her face. She had just slurped down a large, shaved ice with pineapple syrup, adzuki beans, coconut flakes, with a healthy scoop of coconut ice cream. I demurely picked at my small cup of mango shaved ice.

We'd stopped at Diamond Head to get something cold and refreshing, when the shirtless surfer approached us. He was tall and wiry, wearing blue board shorts with a white floral pattern. I figured he was in his early thirties, and he had a killer smile to go along with his killer body.

"Hey, brah... *chill*," Kailani said.

"Sista, why you gotta give me the stink eye? I'm all love." He leaned close to me and whispered huskily in my ear. *"All love."*

I watched them verbally spar in pidgin for a while until lover boy threw his hands up in mock surrender with a chuckle and left.

"Your superpower is definitely attracting horny dudes."

"*Superpower?* I think it's more like a curse."

"Let's face it... you're a *hottie*," she teased.

I shook my head at her. When I looked at my reflection in the mirror, I saw the gawky, flat chested, fifteen-year-old with oily skin and bad acne. I had to wash my face three times daily to feel clean. I wore a 34B bra back then, and I was now a 38D with thirty-eight hips. I had no idea how that happened, but men seemed fascinated by my curvy shape.

I tried not to notice them, gawking at me from the waist up. I covered myself up when I went out, but it didn't seem to deter them. Rodrigo actually said if he had my perfect breasts, he'd feel himself up every day.

I thought Kailani had the ideal physique, petite and lean after years of doing yoga. She had shapely, toned calves.

"Men seem to parse my body parts like I'm a fryer chicken. They seem to either be a breast fan or a leg man," I said.

"Or… a *butt man*!" Kailani answered with a laugh.

I wondered if lesbians did that. I never broached the subject with her. Before she outed herself with her wife Shara, she'd dated men exclusively during college and after.

Then it seemed, one day, she announced she'd fallen in love with a co-worker at the county hospital where she worked as a senior supervisor in the purchasing department. Shara Johnson was a willowy blonde nurse, a recent divorcee with three small children. The news had baffled Cassie and me.

That was fifteen years ago, and they both seemed content with each other, even adventuring to the Big Island years ago. I was impressed how they started their new lives seamlessly. Shara had quickly gotten a nursing job, while Kailani got her yoga teacher certificate. Between her yoga classes and massage bookings on two islands—Oahu and the Big Island, she did pretty well.

Walking back to her big white truck, I reflected that it was such a blessing to be with Kailani again. Her sunny disposition and easy laugh distracted me from my soap opera life back in California.

We drove down Monserrat Street in Diamond Head, heading back to the apartment. The skies were clearing after a brief downpour of tropical rain. The colors were so vivid on the islands—clear turquoise skies, big, puffy, cream-colored clouds hanging lazily above us, and a vertical rainbow magically appeared.

"Look at that!" Kailani said with excitement. I never got tired of her child-like enthusiasm when she saw rainbows. She abruptly pulled over and whipped out her iPhone and started taking pictures. We got back on the road quickly, and before long, we were headed east on the H1 freeway. She put on some music, and the sweet sounds of Jake Shimabukuro's ukelele filled the truck cab. The song was Fields of Gold.

"We played this song at our wedding," I commented, trying to keep the sadness out of my voice.

"I remember. *I was there*. Sweetie, Jason isn't the man you married anymore. I don't know if it was the drinking or what, but you deserve better."

She said this in a matter-of-fact way, but it felt like an accusation that I'd sold myself short.

Which I had… I had to admit to myself I tended to be attracted to emotionally distant men. But Jason had seemed different in the beginning.

As if reading my mind, Kailani said, "At first, he was all over you. *I get it.* But like your therapist said, that energy is more like… being attracted to the attraction and not true love."

Great. Now Kailani is throwing my therapist's advice back at me. I knew she was trying to be helpful, but it stung.

"Everything seemed perfect in the beginning," I replied.

She reached over and patted my hand fondly. "You sweet, sentimental crab. You have to hang on even when it's over."

As soon as we entered the apartment, Kailani flipped on the AC and ceiling fans. I went into the sitting room and flopped down on the sofa. She was in the kitchenette, busy making a fruit salad, cutting fresh bananas, papaya, strawberries, and kiwi fruit. She'd also put on her favorite Jawaiian music playlist and starting grooving to The Manao Company band, swaying and humming as she drizzled honey over the fruit salad. I got up and watched her from the doorway as she started singing the Aloha song. She danced up to me and pulled me close, and we swayed together to the music.

"Spread a little aloha around the world!" she sang.

I absolutely loved this moment. The smell of freshly sliced strawberries permeated the room, mixed with the scent of Kailani's plumeria perfume. She twirled me around as the next song, "A Place in the Sun," started. Suddenly, there was a rap at the front door, and Kailani let go of my hand and hurried down the stairs.

I followed her as she opened the door wide to reveal Cassie Lopez in full beach garb. "Oh my God!" I gasped. We all screamed and fumbled into an awkward group hug.

"What the hell?" I said as we all wiped happy tears from our cheeks.

"It was Cassie's idea to surprise you," Kailani said with a grin.

"You got me. I had no clue… but I'm so glad you're here!" I said.

"I couldn't let you girls have all the fun without me," Cassie said.

She dragged her Louis Vuitton luggage into the foyer, looking super chic in a big black, floppy straw hat, oversized, square Gucci sunglasses, and a purple, halter-top jumpsuit. She smelled of her signature Jo Malone perfume.

"I'm starved!" Cassie said.

***

We got burgers from Teddy's Bigger Burgers back at the Koko Marina shopping center and headed east toward Waimanalo Beach. It was my favorite beach, and Cassie hadn't been, so we decided to eat our lunch there.

Kailani confidently navigated the scenic, winding road toward East Oahu. As we passed the Makupuu lighthouse and the famous blowhole, Cassie gasped in wonder. Kailani turned down a side street off the main road into a non-descript subdivision just one block from the beach.

We unloaded a large beach umbrella, beach towels, and a plastic cooler with drinks, then Kailani led us through a narrow path between houses toward the beach. I caught my breath when we arrived, because the view was stunning. The ocean was a rippling, iridescent, lapis-blue beneath a clear, cloudless sky. We stepped onto warm, powdery, alabaster sand, and I kicked off my flip flops. I heard Cassie gasp and looked over at her with concern. Tears were streaming down her face.

She hurriedly wiped them away with the back of her hand. "This is so *beautiful*."

"You okay?" Kailani asked.

Cassie laughed awkwardly. "I'm just overwhelmed. It's like here we are in this amazing place… all *three* of us. I missed this—just hanging with you guys. No kids, no ex-husbands, no divorce drama…"

Kailani dropped the cooler and hugged her. "You weirdo," she joked.

"Seriously, here we are, forty years later. We were the brown-skinned geek girls who found each other. All of us only children with no siblings or parents. All three of us trying to fit in a place where the popular girls were blonde and thin. We were always the outsiders," Cassie said.

"*You* had parents," I said.

Cassie shrugged. "I hardly saw my father after the divorce. My mother was too busy keeping up with the Jones' to pay much attention to me. Or she was looking for her next husband."

We set up camp close to the water and sat down to eat. There weren't a lot of people around, though I saw two young couples frolicking in the ocean.

Kailani and Cassie were busy catching up, and I was alone with my thoughts. It was a miracle that we'd stayed in contact during the last forty years. Thanks to social media, we'd managed to keep track of each other on Facebook and Instagram. Cassie had the most prolific posts online. She posted almost daily, mainly her everyday routine of working out, eating, and activities with her daughter. Kailani posted occasionally—mainly updates to her growing brood of step-children and pets. I rarely posted.

"I can't believe I just ate that whole burger!" Cassie moaned. She grabbed a bottle of chilled water from the cooler and poured it over her hands. Kailani handed her a paper towel, which she used to briskly dry her hands.

"Messy but worth every bite. I was starved. I didn't eat breakfast or dinner last night!" she added.

"That is so unlike you," I said.

She waved a hand at me, "I always get nervous before a flight, and I had to be at the airport at five-thirty in the morning. I was too busy packing and unpacking last night."

"And fooling around with Montrell, right?" Kailani said.

"*Busted*," Cassie conceded with a laugh.

"Cradle robber!" Kailani said.

"He's got amazing stamina."

"T M I," I said.

"Oh my God, Kai, you used to brag about Giorgio when you were married," Cassie said.

"No, I didn't."

"*You did.* You said you guys never left your room during your honeymoon in Fiji."

"Oh *that*. It was a long time ago."

"And… you never talk about Shara," Cassie said.

"We're good. We've got jam-packed lives—kids, animals, and my massage clients on both islands."

"Isn't it expensive to fly back and forth? Why bother having clients in Honolulu?"

Kailani rubbed her thumb and index fingers together.

"*Big bucks* here. I can charge double for a couples' massage in Waikiki hotels. It's cheap to fly back and forth. Besides, I only do it once a month."

"My mom's got hip replacement surgery scheduled when I get back. My brother is conveniently back in rehab. He lives rent free with her, and he can't be bothered to help nurse her when she gets out of the hospital. UGH… *family*!" Cassie turned to me and said, "You're so lucky you don't have family drama."

"My whole family's dead. So, not an issue," I replied.

"Jesus, Cassie, can you be more insensitive?" Kailani said.

Cassie's hands flew to her mouth. "I'm so sorry. I didn't mean it like that."

I put my arm around her. "It's all good. I've always had this existential loneliness since childhood. I've gotten used to it."

"*We're* your family," Kailani said.

"I know that," I said. "It's just… the last twenty years, Jason was my family. I'm just in this weird in-between state, and I don't know what's going to happen with Rodrigo and me. And now I'll probably be moving and looking for a job when I get back."

"Oh, Sweetie, it'll be okay," Cassie rubbed my back. "You can always stay with me… I've got plenty of room."

"And you can always come stay with Shara and me. The kids would love having you," Kailani added.

I appreciated their kindnesses, but they both had their own complicated lives, with elderly parents, children, work, and animals. I'd just be a third wheel, and I realized I'd felt that way my entire life until I got married. Jason and I had created a life together, which had blessed me with stability and belonging. I didn't crave the busyness that my two best friends seemed to be enmeshed in. I wanted to confidently plan a future, but I didn't even know where to start.

"Come on, let's get wet!" Kailani said. She sprang up, pulled off her long, black, lacy, beach cover-up dress, revealing a red, one-piece swimsuit.

"I'm good," Cassie said. "I need to sit and digest."

"Same," I said.

Kailani shrugged and jogged down to the water and dove in. She bobbed up a few minutes later and gave us a cheerful thumbs up sign.

"I think she's part mermaid," Cassie said. "And part Baywatch babe."

I nodded. "Actually, I'm on my period and don't want to get wet."

"You're still having cycles?" Cassie asked with surprise.

I nodded.

"I still have some spotting. I sure don't miss the horrific cramps. Ugh."

We watched Kailani serenely floating on her back like an otter. The two frolicking couples were drying off nearby, slathering on suntan lotion. I envied their carefree demeanor as they joked and sipped bottled water. Cassie followed my wistful gaze and patted my hand.

"This too shall pass."

***

Later that evening, Kailani went off to Waikiki, since she had massage bookings, so it was just Cassie and I having dinner near the Gold Coast. The setting sun was a golden crescent disappearing into the silvery-blue, undulating ocean. Coral and ochre clouds streaked the sky as the final embers of sunlight faded from view.

We listened to the relaxing Waikiki surf as we lingered over plates of garlic shrimp and salad at the Barefoot Beach Café near Queens Beach. We sat at a white wooden table underneath a wood portico. Strings of small bright lights lit up the patio outside. It was normally crowded with tourists, but it turned out to be a mellow evening with about half the tables occupied. Cassie was scarfing down the last of her fries, sipping a bottle of Sierra Nevada IPA beer we brought from the house, while I savored my root beer float.

"Ugh, I shouldn't have gotten the fries, I feel gross," Cassie said with a sigh.

"You seemed to enjoy every bite," I said.

"They were delicious, but now I need some water." She got up and gestured toward the glass water pitchers to the side of the restaurant. "You want a glass?"

"Sure, thanks."

I checked my phone for messages and saw Rodrigo had texted me a silly picture of himself and Kiki sticking their tongues out. *I miss him.*

A commotion in front of me interrupted my musing, and I looked up to see a black crow pecking at Cassie's leftover fries. I clapped my hands loudly to scare him away, but he just stared at me.

"*Shoo!*" I said.

I heard someone behind me and looked up to see a white-haired woman with a dishrag. She snapped the cloth at the bird and shouted. The crow looked irritated but took off. She turned toward me and laughed, reminding me of Lulu with her spikey white hair and colorful muumuu dress.

"That *alala* was so greedy!"

"I've never seen a crow on the island before," I said.

She shrugged. "When I was a girl, they were everywhere, but no more. When the *alala* shows himself, it means an ancestor is sending you a message."

"What kind of message?"

She shrugged and grinned impishly and shuffled away as Cassie returned with plastic cups of water.

"What was that all about?"

"A crow landed on your fries. That woman saved the rest of your meal."

"You and your obsession with crows!"

"I'm not obsessed. They just seem to stalk me wherever I am."

"I read an article about the Hawaiian crows on the plane. They're extinct on the islands… you must have seen a blackbird," Cassie said. "Between you and Kai… her whole *'I see dead people'* vibe." She shuddered.

I heard my phone ping and looked down to see another text from Rodrigo. It was a kiss emoji. I showed Cassie, who nodded in approval.

"Any word from Jason… since the hookup?"

I shook my head. "I don't know what I was thinking. Clearly, I wasn't."

"Hey, there's nothing like sex with the ex-husband. So, I get it."

"You have any regrets about hooking up with Steve in Disneyland? That turned out not so good."

"Not my best moment. I didn't expect the kiddo to walk in during the night."

"So, you didn't have any feelings for him after that?

Cassie tilted her head to one side. "Not really. I was just craving his cock. I don't think I told you, but he's the biggest I've ever been with. *Huge.*"

She *had* told me before. What was embarrassing was she'd told both Kailani and me when she started dating him, and after that, that's all I could think about when I saw him. Cassie sipped her water and checked her phone.

"Check out this text from Montrell."

I looked over to see a photograph of her handsome, young, black boyfriend at the gym wearing a snug red tank top and flexing his biceps.

"He's coming out in two days!" Cassie said happily.

"I thought you were hanging with us this week on the Big Island."

"I *am*. He's not coming for two whole days. He's never been to Maui, so it'll be fun. You guys should take a happy hop and come and join us. That's the fun of being here—each island is just a thirty minute happy hop away!"

"I'm good with staying on the Big Island for now."

Cassie jumped up. "Let's do a selfie so I can post on Instagram."

Before I could react, she pressed her face next to mine and snapped. I looked at her phone and saw two middle-aged women grinning beneath a velvety, charcoal, night sky, their windblown hair swirling around their smiling faces.

Chapter Eleven

The most tedious part of flying was sitting as a captive audience at the airline gate. You are subjected to snippets of loud, inane cell phone conversation that you can't escape from. Seats at the gate seem to fill up quickly, and people randomly mill around with noisy children, or worse, have even louder conversations on speaker mode on their cell phones.

Jason and I used to play a game, which entailed spotting the most horribly dressed tourist. I shared this with Cassie, who, despite looking pale and hungover, agreed to participate.

"*There!*" I said.

A chubby, pale woman wearing an orange caftan with black and orange knee socks and brown hiking boots passed us with her oversized backpack. As she got closer, I noticed small Halloween pumpkins on the socks.

Cassie smirked and shook her head and pointed out a man sitting near us. "*Him*!" she said.

He looked middle-aged, probably mid-to-late forties. He wore a black and silver Raiders football cap and a black t-shirt that read, "*I got crabs in San Francisco.*" He also wore khaki cargo shorts, white knee socks, and leather Birkenstock sandals.

"Sorry, but I think pumpkin lady wins over Raiders fan," I said.

Cassie rolled her eyes. "I shouldn't have had that third cocktail," she moaned.

"So, what did Montrell text you about last night?"

"Nothing important." Cassie lowered her oversized sunglasses over her eyes. She was dressed in a denim, short sleeved romper with matching blue denim platform sandals. Her hair was neatly tucked under a red Los Angeles Dodgers baseball cap.

"My head hurts," she moaned. "And I'm having the mother-of-all hot flashes!" She futilely fanned herself with her paper boarding pass.

"I only had *one,* and I felt it right away."

Cassie rolled her eyes, "You're such a lightweight."

"Jason always called me a *cheap date*."

"Yeah because you put out after just one drink. Hey, remind me again who Diana is?"

I sighed impatiently. I had my moments of brain fog going through perimenopause, but Cassie took it to another level. In the past, I'd wondered if she had undiagnosed ADHD.

"You met her at Kailani's wedding. She owns the yoga retreat place we're staying at in Hilo."

Cassie shook her head. "If I did, I can't remember. Besides, that was ten years ago. I can barely remember what we ate for dinner last night. And I'm not part of the *wahine* club like you, Kai, and Diana."

"It's not a club. We happen to stay in touch regularly because of the yoga retreat."

I took out my phone and scrolled through my photo gallery, pulling up Kailani's wedding pictures. I found one with the four of us—Kailani, Diana, Cassie, and me, showing it to Cassie, who frowned.

"She doesn't look familiar."

"Diana and her sister bought the retreat site right around the time when Kailani and Shara got married. It was in foreclosure and in pretty bad shape. It took them forever, but they remodeled the lodge and put up cabins. Believe it or not, they did most of the work. Diana documented the remodeling on her Facebook page. You should check it out."

"Uh huh." Cassie was busy scrolling through her iPhone.

"I stayed there twice while they were re-building. The second time, Shara, Kailani, and the kids stayed there too. Remember when the volcano blew six years ago? Their house got seriously gassed, so they hunkered down with Diana and ended up staying. It was a win-win since they live and work there for free."

"Good for them," Cassie murmured.

"You don't follow Diana on Facebook?"

Cassie shook her head.

I vividly remembered staying in a primitive hut during the second phase of their rebuilding. It was barely bigger than a garden tool shed, with a corrugated metal roof and a camping cot. When it rained, the noise on the metal roof was thunderous.

"What's going on? You seem preoccupied," I asked Cassie.

"Oh nothing. Steve wants to keep Celestina an extra week. His parents want to take her on a road trip to their place in Baja."

"*Tijuana?*"

"No, they have a vacation home in San Felipe."

"Sounds nice."

"Whatever. " She shrugged.

What was going on with her? A pre-boarding announcement was made, followed quickly by an announcement for regular boarding. Pumpkin Lady got up, boarding ahead of us in first class. She smirked at me as she passed by.

***

"Is this… *it?*" Cassie looked out the window. It had been an uneventful, quick flight over from Honolulu to the Big Island.

She lowered her sunglasses and peered out the plane window at the modest Kona airport, fanning herself with a paper vomit bag folded in half. During the forty-minute flight, she'd said little.

I thought about her change of mood after we'd met Kailani at Duke's bar in Waikiki after dinner the previous night. It'd turned dour after receiving numerous texts from her ex-husband, Celestina, and Montrell. I had gotten one text from Rodrigo—a video clip of Tracy Chapman's hit "The Promise." Listening to the lyrics about patiently waiting for me with love in his heart made my eyes fill with tears. My throat closed up as I thought about his text.

Cassie reached into her purse and pulled out a gold-toned compact mirror, then stared critically at her reflection. "God, I should have put on some concealer. My eyes are so baggy. So, what's Diana like?"

"Diana's fun and upbeat. Very... granola Earth Mama type."

"She sounds interesting." Cassie put her mirror away and peered out the window. "Isn't there a jetway? How do we get down *there*?"

The Kona airport was a cozy, open-air airport with only eleven gates. There was no jetway, so deplaning meant disembarking on a portable ramp onto the tarmac. Cassie got up and grabbed her carry-on luggage from the overhead bin. I reached for my backpack, which I'd managed to tuck under the seat in front of me.

"How did you fit all your stuff in that?" Cassie asked.

I shrugged. "I've always traveled light. You basically only need tank tops, shorts, and flip flops here."

We shuffled off the plane in an orderly fashion, with Cassie pressing on in front of me down the ramp. She took small, mincing steps in her platform shoes. When we got on the tarmac, she glanced around.

"This is so basic," she said.

We made our way through the baggage claim area to the front of the airport, where we were supposed to meet Diana. Kailani had taken an earlier flight to get the property ready for our visit as well as to teach a yoga class. She had made arrangements with Diana, who was already in town to pick us up.

We'd decided to fly into Kona instead of Hilo to spend the day sightseeing, and made our way past the baggage claim section toward the curb. I checked my phone and saw a text from Diana confirming she was circling the airport in her gray Kia Soul. I turned to Cassie.

"Diana's here already. Look for a gray Kia Soul."

"*A what?*"

"Never mind—I think that's her pulling up."

We both looked up in time to see a boxy, gray, SUV pull up near the curb. Diana jumped out and waved both arms in the air to get our attention. Her stocky body was cloaked in a short, brown, velour muumuu, a white Plumeria blossom tucked behind one ear, and black Croc sandals. She had a round, tanned face creased with wrinkles and an easy smile, her dome-shaped head clean shaven like a Tibetan nun.

"*Howzit?*"

It surprised me to hear Diana's New York City accented pidgin English. We hugged and I gestured toward Cassie.

"You remember Cassie?" I said.

"Aloha!" Diana said. "We met at Kai's wedding."

"So I'm told," Cassie said. "Sorry… but I am in dire need of coffee." She smiled sweetly at Diana.

"There's a McDonald's nearby," Diana said.

"I don't do McDonalds. Isn't there a Starbucks close by? I'm craving an Oleato."

"Sure… no problem."

Diana arched an eyebrow and glanced over at me as she grabbed Cassie's carry-on. I hauled my backpack to the back of the car and loaded it inside, leaning over to whisper, "Cassie will be okay once she's caffeinated."

Diana nodded. "So, besides coffee… what's your pleasure? I'm your Uber for the day!" Diana said cheerfully.

Cassie got in the back, while I slipped into the passenger side next to Diana.

"We're open to suggestions," I said.

"Kai thought a drive to Captain Cook would be nice. There's a beach near there where you can see turtles and dolphins. I've got snorkeling gear in back with beach towels if you feel like getting wet."

"Sounds great," I said.

I glanced at the rear view mirror and noticed Cassie busy texting.

"That sound good, Cassie?"

She silently nodded as she continued to text. *What is going on with her?*

***

Two Step beach near Captain Cook was a favorite local snorkeling spot. I helped Diana with hauling a canvas beach bag, beach chairs, towels, and a cooler with bottled water onto the sand. We scooted past a flock of clucking feral chickens that darted in front of us. Cassie was still sitting in the car, sipping her Starbucks Oleato and texting.

Diana looked over her shoulder at her. "Is she okay?" she asked. She set up the beach chairs near the water.

I shrugged. "I know she woke up with a massive hangover. I'm not sure what all the texting is about… that's not her usual style."

"By the way, thanks for the coffee, I couldn't believe how expensive it was. McDonald's coffee suits my budget."

"You're welcome. I wasn't a big coffee drinker until I got married. Jason got me hooked with his special blend. He'd make me a cup every morning in a French press," I wistfully recalled our cozy, late mornings in bed. I'd wake up to the tantalizing smell of freshly brewed coffee. I missed his crab benedict that he'd serve with his special homemade hollandaise sauce.

"I didn't know Jason very well, but the few times we interacted, I thought he was a real gentleman."

Diana's comment snapped me out of my sentimental reverie. "Thanks for saying that."

"I know things didn't go well at the end, but he was a good listener and seemed to really care about you."

"I know. It was great in the beginning. I'd say the first ten years it felt like we were on a non-stop honeymoon. He was tender and loving. Then he got obsessed with his restaurant, and he was spending more time there with his business partner, Candace, than me. Every day there was always a crisis."

My cheeks burned thinking about Candace and her constant urgent texts.

"Look, my AA sponsor used to say people come for a reason, a season, or a lifetime. Unfortunately, Jason came for a season. Rodrigo sounds like a good person. Be happy you found someone special." It was a strange coincidence that Dr. Serena had said that earlier.

"He's so much younger than me. I don't know if he'll stick around either."

"Listen, honey, at our age, we gotta live in the moment. Tomorrow isn't guaranteed. Be thankful you found someone who cares so much about you."

"You're right. By the way, you look good… island life suits you. Are you still working at the rehab clinic?"

"I've finally found my happy place. I love the wildness and unpredictable feeling of being here. Nope, I quit. I took early social security. My sister and I pooled our finances together to buy the yoga retreat property. Hey, Kai said you finally got your money back."

"I did."

My chest tightened with sadness. *I got the money and now it's finally done. There's no reason to stay in touch with him.*

Cassie screamed, and I looked up to see her frozen in place in the parking lot, her hands clamped over her mouth, her eyes bugged out with fright.

"What's wrong, honey?" Diana jumped to her feet.

"There was… a *rat*!"

I got up, and we walked over to the parking lot.

"It was probably a mongoose," Diana said. She rubbed Cassie's arm and tried to calm her down.

"And what's with all these *chickens*?"

Diana chuckled, "They're harmless. They're feral chickens… they're rampant all over the island."

"*Oh great!*"

"Come over to the water and relax," I said.

She let Diana guide her by the hand over to our beach chairs, where Cassie plunked down on my chair and sighed. She reached into her handbag and pulled out a tube of sunscreen.

Diana leaned over and said, "That's reef safe, right? You gotta be careful what you put on your skin these days."

Cassie shrugged. "I got it at Sephora,"

Diana opened her beach bag and pulled out a purple tube of sunscreen.

"Try this stuff out. No bad chemicals, only zinc oxide. Thing about it… they say that the nasty chemical sunscreen is killing the reef. Yet we slather that stuff on our bodies!"

Cassie looked at Diana like she sprouted a second head. But she took the purple tube and began to slather herself. Diana smiled with satisfaction.

I turned toward Cassie. "Is everything okay back home? You seem preoccupied," I asked.

Cassie threw her hands up. "There's always drama with my family, and now Montrell is saying he needs personal space. *What the hell*?"

"What does *that* mean?"

Cassie shook her head irately, "*I don't know!*"

"Sorry, Cassie. He *is* young… maybe he just needs…"

Before I could finish, she blurted out, "I don't want to talk about it. I'm going for a swim."

She kicked off her shoes, pulled off her romper, revealing her black, two-piece thong bikini, and sprinted over to the water and plunged in. Diana raised her eyebrows and looked at me. "That's exactly why I swore off men years ago. Been celibate for five years now… been the happiest I've been for a while."

Maybe Diana was onto something?

Chapter Twelve

We made it to Kailani and Shara's yoga retreat home by sunset. Diana navigated the SUV down a wide, rocky driveway and parked in front of the main building.

The lodge was wood shingled, with a peaked green roof. Amber lights illuminated the main building, while bright motion sensor lights lit up the path leading to the front wooden doors. It felt good to get out of the car and stretch our legs.

We were met with the loud chirping noise of mating coqui frogs, which reverberated throughout the darkness. Cassie had perked up somewhat, but her continued lapses into silence made me wonder if Montrell's text had really upset her more than she disclosed.

A pack of barking dogs charged down the driveway as Diana and I unloaded the luggage. I recognized Kailani's long-haired *Chiweenie* dog, Ozzie, from her Instagram posts. The other long-haired wiener dogs whined and circled us. Cassie was still in the backseat and was hesitant to get out.

I heard Kailani's voice as she came out of the lodge and called off the dogs. Ozzie turned toward her and ran straight into her arms. She scooped him up and kissed his nose.

"Welcome, ladies!" She put Ozzie down and hugged Diana and me. "I hope you guys are hungry. I made a ton of food!" Kailani said.

She looked over at Cassie, who finally got out and was eyeing Ozzie suspiciously.

"He doesn't bite," Kailani said.

"Sorry, but I desperately need to use the bathroom, and I probably need a shower too. Are the rooms ready?" Cassie said.

"You have a choice of a lodge room with a private bath or a cabin with a shared bath,"

"Cassie can have the lodge room," I said.

Cassie smiled gratefully at me and retrieved her overnight bag.

"I'll take you there," Kailani said.

We watched as the two of them headed off, then Diana gestured toward the lodge kitchen nearby. "I'll make us some ice teas while m'lady refreshes herself."

I followed her to a green building to the left of the main lodge, past a beige canvas canopy-shaded outdoor dining area. I had forgotten how loud the coqui frogs sounded at night—like crickets on steroids. The air was also pretty humid, and it felt like walking through a steamy sauna. Inside the kitchen there was a long, Koa wood dining table topped with bowls and platters of vegan food. There was also a stack of white ceramic plates and a wicker basket of silverware wrapped inside white cloth napkins. The kitchen smelled of savory spices, which made the space feel homey and cozy. I detected the pleasing fresh scent of lemongrass.

Diana swept her hand at the table and announced, "Sesame noodle salad with smoked tofu, grilled butternut squash with garlic butter and pomegranate seeds, mixed green salad, and toasted spelt pita wraps. Also, there's miso soup on the stove." She went to the 'fridge and stuck her head inside. "Kai beat me to the punch… there's ice tea already made."

She pulled out a frosted glass pitcher and grabbed three glasses from the sink. We sat down at the corner of the table, and Kailani came in as Diana was pouring out the tea.

"What's up with Cassie? She's in a serious funk," Kailani said.

"She woke up with a hangover, and I guess there's some drama with Montrell going on," I replied.

Kailani shook her head and sat at the table. I took a sip of the ice tea.

"There's something else going on," Kailani said. "I can *feel* it."

"She perked up a little after she went for a swim, but she's been mostly quiet," I said.

"We saw some turtles at the beach, and it didn't even faze her." Diana added.

"We stopped at Longs on the way over so she could buy some Advil and sunscreen," I added.

We were all seated at the table, facing each other.

"You really put out an amazing spread of food," I said.

"There's a couple staying at one of the cabins, so there's six of us for dinner. But I haven't seen them all day. You guys should eat… I don't think Cassie's going to make it. She sat down on the bed and then passed out," Kailani said.

"You don't have to ask me twice!" Diana got up, and I followed her lead and picked up a plate. Kailani was a fantastic vegan chef, and while she was an omnivore, she acquiesced to Shara's desire to maintain a meat-free household. It was mostly for the children's sake. I hadn't realized how hungry I was until we walked into the kitchen.

***

Cassie didn't show up until after nine that evening. She shuffled into the kitchen wearing a short, light-blue onesie with spaghetti straps and plunked down at the table with a sigh. Her eyes were puffy, and her hair was mussed up as though she'd just staggered out of bed.

"Look who's returned to the land of the living!" Diana joked.

I got up and got a glass of ice tea for her. She gulped down the entire glass while I stood there.

"I'm so thirsty," she moaned.

"How're you feeling?" Kailani asked.

Cassie shook her head. "Like *shit*."

"I've got some Advil in the pantry if you need some more," Kailani said.

Cassie sighed. "I'm good."

"So, what's going on?" I asked.

Cassie put her hands over her face, sniffled, and blurted out, "I'm *pregnant!*"

"Are you serious?" Kailani said.

Cassie rubbed her eyes. "I am serious. The worst part is I don't know who the father is."

"What does *that* mean?" I asked.

"It's probably Montrell's... but it could also be—"

"Your ex-husband?" Diana said.

Cassie nodded slowly. Her face was tear streaked and pale.

"I got a pregnancy test when I was at Longs," Cassie explained.

So, that's why she was so quiet.

There was an awkward silence as we all digested the unexpected information. I got up and refilled Cassie's glass just so I had something to do. Kailani followed my lead and started a dinner plate for Cassie. She scooped some sesame noodles on a clean plate, when Cassie waved her off.

"That's plenty. I don't really have an appetite."

Kailani put the plate in front of her along with a cloth napkin and fork, then over and hugged her from behind.

"Don't worry, we'll figure this out, Sweetie."

Cassie burst into fresh tears at Kailani's touch.

"I totally fucked up. I can't believe it… I didn't think I could get pregnant since I'm practically menopausal. It's all my fault—I never made Montrell wear a condom, and then Steve and I had a quickie at his parents' house last month when I dropped off Celestina. Oh my God, what a shit show," she wailed.

I patted Cassie's shoulder. " Kailani's right… we're here for you. You don't have to figure this out right this minute. Maybe you got a false positive? It happens."

Cassie sniffled. "I love you guys so much."

"Like the song says, *that's what friends are for!*" Diana said.

Cassie smiled faintly. Diana was right, we'd figure it out together.

Chapter Thirteen

I got up and reached for my diary and re-read an entry I'd jotted down.

"I see Lono swimming in the ocean, and he disappears under the waves. Then he bobs back up, but he's turned into a sea turtle."

I wondered what the dream meant. I'd awakened drenched in sweat and had the disquieting feeling that I was being watched. Sometimes, it seemed like the jungle surrounding the property came alive after dark. Tonight, the full moon bathed the meadow in an eerie, phosphorescent light. When I woke up, I thought someone was shining a bright flashlight through the cabin window. When I got out of bed to investigate, I opened the door and saw the deserted meadow illuminated, the rhythmic sound of the coqui frogs filling the night. Then I heard whispering voices but couldn't see anyone.

Kailani had told me once she'd seen *menehunes* as a child, fabled and elusive dwarves that were thought to live furtively in the wilderness.

Adding to my sense of unease was a cryptic text from Blake I'd received after dinner requesting I call him right away. A ripple of worry caused my stomach to clench. Blake used to pre-emptively text me from the restaurant when Jason was coming home in a bad mood. Strangely, the same anxiety pulsed in my body. *What could possibly be going on?* It'd been too late to return his call.

I returned to bed and tried to shake off my anxious thoughts.

In the morning, I peered through the cabin windows and noticed the sun peeking through fluffy white clouds. The only place to get reception was in the middle of the forty acre property near the Kwan Yin statue.

I looked down at my phone and saw I had one bar. I opened the front door of the cabin and slipped on my flip flops. My sandals made squishy sounds on the wet grass as I headed to the statue. In minutes, I was standing next to the tall, cement Kwan Yin sculpture, the benevolent Buddhist goddess wearing a permanently tranquil expression, with lowered eyes and a peaceful smile. She towered over me, her hands clasped in prayer. Kwan Yin was always referred to as the goddess of compassion, and her serene expression was comforting. Miraculously, I now had two bars, so I called Blake. He picked up immediately.

"Hey, babe. How's island life?"

"Soggy. I'm on the big island, and it's raining pretty good. I got your text, what's up?"

"You're not going to believe this, but Jason is headed your way."

"*Here?*"

"Yep. He wants to make things right with you. He said he blew it, not reining in Candace and all that."

"Does he actually know where I am? I haven't even talked to him."

"He looked up Cassie on Instagram and saw a picture of Kai's yoga retreat. You guys are in Hilo, right?"

I groaned inwardly. *Cassie and her insatiable need to post everything twenty-four seven!*

"Thanks for the warning. How are you doing?"

"I'm good. By the way, one of my workout clients is a big mucky muck at an investment firm. He's looking for a personal assistant. It'd pay *six figures* including the annual bonus. He's a cool dude… you interested? I can set you guys up."

"Thanks… I need to think about it.

"That's cool. Maybe…"

"*Blake*?"

The connection abruptly dropped. I looked down at my phone and saw only one bar. *Great.*

Glancing around the empty paddock, I wondered if the previous evening had all been a weird dream, quickly deciding to head to the kitchen to get a cup of tea and see what Kailani was up to.

Blake's mention of work made me realize I had to start thinking about job interviews as soon as I got back to California. I still had a chunk of savings, but I didn't like to cut things too close money-wise. I hadn't worked a fulltime job in ten years, not counting the administrative work I did for the restaurant since I didn't get paid.

I thought wistfully of my previous pampered housewife life. I had lived in a beautiful townhouse near San Francisco with a view of the Golden Gate Bridge. My daily routine had consisted of sleeping in, walking my dog, and helping out at fundraisers at the animal shelter. It seemed like that was a lifetime ago.

The retreat grounds were eerily deserted. Diana and Cassie had left early to drive out to Rainbow Falls... I'd just missed them at breakfast.

I walked past the community garden, where a flock of white geese were milling around, softly squawking. They ignored me as I passed them and stepped through the back door of the kitchen.

Kailani was chatting on a portable landline phone while chopping up vegetables. There was a big wooden bowl with baby lettuce, cherry tomatoes, and mizuna stems on the long dining table. She waved at me cheerfully when I came in.

"It's Shara... say hello." She held out the phone.

"Hey, Shara, how's it going?"

"Great. I'm sorry I can't be there to see you. It's been *ages*."

"When are you coming back? Hopefully soon?"

"I'm *trying*. My mother's doing better, and the kids love being here to visit their *Nana*, so making the most of it."

"Well, I miss you. Kailani's doing a great job cooking and keeping us in line."

"You enjoying healthy, *meat-free* meals?"

I glanced over at Kailani, who rolled her eyes in amusement. I heard someone's voice saying something to Shara. There was a brief whispered conversation, and Shara said, "Sorry, I gotta run, the kiddos are hungry. See you when I see you two. *Love you both*."

Kailani shook her head and put the phone down on the marble kitchen counter. "Shara is a dedicated animal rights activist. Absolutely no meat products in this house."

"But you love burgers. I couldn't do it."

"You pick your battles, right? Can you put out the ice tea please?" she asked.

I didn't realize it was already lunchtime. There were only two guests on the property—a young Japanese couple on their honeymoon who I'd met at breakfast the other day. They came early and got breakfast trays and headed back to their bright blue cabin across the meadow from me.

"How's Cassie this morning?" I asked.

"Thanks to Diana, I think she's doing better. She went to check on her, and they stayed up late talking. Those pregnancy kits aren't foolproof. Cassie's going to do a blood test when she gets back to the Bay Area. If she *is* pregnant, she's going to talk to Steve. She's now thinking about the timing, and it's most likely Steve."

"Please clue me in. I thought she and Montrell were solid."

She shrugged. "She could never resist Steve. Remember back in high school when he was captain of the football team? Cassie had the biggest crush on him."

"Yep, but he was dating that blonde cheerleader," I said. "*Ashley.*"

"Tall, blonde, and perfect," I added.

She nodded. "Cassie became obsessed with him. She even signed up for a charity walkathon so she could stalk him."

"Wow. I didn't know that. I'm not judging Cassie—I mean, considering I just slept with my own ex-husband before the ink was dry on the paperwork. Speaking of ex-husbands, I just found out that Jason is headed here."

I told her what Blake had said, and she sighed, finished chopping up an English cucumber, and tossed it in the salad bowl. She wiped her hands on a cotton dish rag as I took the ice tea pitcher out of the refrigerator and put it on the table.

"He better not show up. The ancestors don't want him around. I just heard them say that."

"We'll set the dogs on him if he shows up… that'll teach him!" I added.

"Don't worry about Jason. The ancestors are watching over you."

"Well, I wish they'd sent me smoke signals."

"They always tell me we have *free will*. They can advise but they can't interfere. Besides, a while back, your therapist warned you that Jason might pop back into your life, remember? You even texted me about it."

"You're *right*."

We sat down at the serving table, and Kailani poured us each a glass of plantation tea—a mixture of black tea, pineapple juice, and agave syrup. I sipped and I told her about the dream about Lono turning into a sea turtle.

"What do you think it means?" I asked.

"The *honu* are sacred to many indigenous beliefs," she said. "There are many stories about *turtle island*... that the Earth was formed on the back of a turtle. There's even a Hindu story about Vishnu reincarnating as a turtle named *Kachhapa* that carried the weight of the world on its back."

"Does Lono have a connection with the *honu*?"

"The turtles sure seem to show up when he's out swimming. I call him the turtle whisperer! In fact, Lono is out back, near the meditation yurt doing landscaping, you should go say hello."

"Sure, it'd be fun to see him."

"He'll be happy to see you."

I finished my ice tea and got up. As the screen door to the kitchen slammed shut behind me, I wondered what to expect. Except for spontaneous Facebook video chats when Kailani and I were hanging out, I hadn't seen him in real life for a long time.

The meditation yurt was a ten minute walk away. The air was warm, but the humidity was mild, and it felt nice to be outside. Only the lodge rooms had air conditioning.

The path was lined with verdant hapu'u fern trees, spikey red and yellow aechmea blanchetiana bromeliad plants, and bright cerise ti plants with feathery, slender leaves. There were no shade trees along the path, and the intense sunlight on my bare arms and legs caused my skin to heat up.

Up ahead, the large, round, beige, domed yurt loomed. It reminded me of a documentary I saw on nomadic Mongolian tribes. To the side of the yurt stood a tall, slender, bronzed man rinsing himself off with a garden hose. He was completely naked, with his bare, pale buttocks exposed. The only accessory he had on was his black Giants baseball cap. Thank God his back was to me. My face went hot. I stopped walking several yards away, and called out.

"Hey… *Lono!*"

"Hey *Sista*!"

To my relief, he whipped off his baseball hat and covered his pelvic region as he turned around.

"I wasn't expecting anyone," Lono said with a boyish grin. "I thought the honeymooners checked out."

"I think they're still here."

"My clothes and beach towel are inside. Be back in a second."

Before I could answer, he abruptly vanished inside the yurt. I moved closer to the tent and stood on the stairs. Lono reappeared fully clothed in a gray Giant's tank top with the familiar orange and black SF logo, denim cutoff shorts, and black flip flops. His face was tanned and already fairly lined from being outdoors year-round. He leaned forward and hugged me.

"So good to see you, *Noelani*," he said.

"It's been a while."

Lono began a series of stretches as we chatted. First he extended his arms over his head, gripped his wrist, and arched to one side and then the other. Then he swung his arms in front of his chest like a windmill.

"So good to have you back to the islands. Sorry, but I'm stiff from gardening all morning."

"I'm just visiting."

"*Maybe.*"

He smiled impishly, giving off that same mysterious, other-worldly vibe that Kailani emanated..

"Come on inside, it's cooler." He gestured for me to follow inside the yurt.

The interior was surprisingly cool and roomy, with a high, peaked ceiling. I stepped onto a clean, hardwood floor, and the room smelled faintly of perfumed incense. A simple Lord Ganesh altar faced the entrance. The elephant god sat comfortably atop a low teak wood meditation table. Next to him was a glass bowl of plumeria blossoms, with glass votive candle holders on each side of the famous demi-god. Near the altar were stacks of round meditation pillows and folded, striped, Mexican, yoga blankets.

Lono grabbed two pillows and sat down on one in front of the altar. I followed suit and stared at the four-armed elephant demi-god. A peacefulness permeated the space, which I found soothing. I was also trying not to stare at Lono. I still couldn't believe he was the scrawny boy who came to San Francisco during the summers to stay with Kailani and their grandmother.

"You're coming to Kailani's full moon meditation tonight, right?"

"I will, but she didn't say anything to me."

"She probably thought you already knew. She does one every full moon and every new moon. She calls in the ancestors for healing and messages."

"That should be interesting!"

"That's putting it mildly," he chuckled.

"She spontaneously gives me messages sometimes—like this morning." I told him about Jason.

"You'll be fine. The ancestors don't want him to disturb you. They will handle it."

Lono said this matter-of-factly. I'd known Kailani for almost forty five years, so I'd grown accustomed to her spontaneous prognostications. It never made sense to question her predictions.

"I had a funny dream about you turning into a *honu*," I said.

"Well, I *am* part honu," he said with a smile.

"I guess that makes sense," I joked.

"I guess Kailani didn't tell you about the time I almost drowned? I was swimming alone at Carlsmith Beach in Hilo... not one of my best decisions since I'd been drinking. I got foot cramps and panicked. I was thrashing around, feeling like a dumb ass because I should have known better. The next thing I knew, a honu appeared, and I grabbed onto him. He got me safely back to the beach."

"That's quite a story,"

"Then he appeared to me in a dream and informed me that my ancestors revered honus and even served as guardians, so he was sent to rescue me."

"You were so lucky,"

"No, *sista*, it wasn't luck. I owe my life to the turtles. They are my tribe."

He smiled enigmatically, and there was a flash of mischief in his dark eyes.

"I'm beginning to think I belong to the crow tribe. They seem to keep popping up everywhere."

"They could simply be a messenger. Native people consider them magical for traveling between the worlds of the living and the dead. My grandfather often saw crows and said they symbolized that change was coming."

I flashed back to the old woman at the outdoor restaurant on Oahu. How she had also smiled mysteriously when the crow appeared.

Lono was saying something, and I looked up. "Sorry, what'd you say?"

"I'm starving. Skipped breakfast to get some gardening done early. Shall we head back?"

We put back the pillows, and I followed Lono out. I had an ominous feeling about the evening meditation—and I wondered what the ancestors had to say.

Chapter Fourteen

It's easy to lose track of time when you're on the Big Island. When evening arrived, I felt like the day had evaporated after talking to Lono earlier. After lunch, I returned to my cabin to read and dozed off.

It was already dark when I got up, and realized I was going to be late for Kailani's full moon meditation if I didn't hustle. I stepped outside and put on my flip flops, startled by how quiet it was. No coqui frog sounds. As I hurried along the path to the meditation yurt, I again had the strange sensation that someone or something was watching me. Goosebumps rippled over both my arms.

I was relieved when I arrived at the yurt and saw several pairs of flip flops outside the front door. When I walked in, I was surprised to see everyone sitting in a semi-circle facing the candlelit Ganesh altar, with Kailani facing outward toward the door. The smell of a sage smudge stick perfumed the room.

Lono, Diana, Cassie, the Japanese honeymooners, and even Ozzie, Kailani's dog, sat silently on meditation pillows. Ozzie seemed to eye me reprovingly as I sat down on a meditation pillow next to Kailani. Everyone had their eyes closed, while Kailani made haunting music with her crystal Tibetan singing bowl. She began to softly chant the *Gayatri Mantra*: *"Om bhur bhuva swaha."* She began to gently sway as she chanted.

I closed my eyes and let the sound travel through me. My muscles relaxed as I focused on Kailani's voice. The sensation of being watched percolated up again, and I opened my eyes and saw a big, white dog silhouetted in the doorway. Ozzie emitted a low, rumbling growl. When I looked back at the doorway, there was nothing there.

A breeze swept through the room, and I became chilled. Kailani stopped chanting and a hush descended inside the yurt, before a blast of cold air whipped through the door, and Ozzie jumped to his feet and began pacing. Something *whooshed* past me, and I heard the sound of light footsteps. An unsettling prickling feeling fanned through me. Ozzie jumped into my lap, shivering and whimpering while I stroked his back to calm him.

"The ancestors are here," Kailani whispered.

Ozzie looked up at me, his limpid, chestnut-brown eyes staring at me with worry, then he burrowed snugly against me.

"It's okay, Ozzie," I said.

I noticed that the honeymooners and Cassie had abruptly left. Only Lono, Diana, Kailani, and I were left sitting in the still, candlelit room. Ozzie began snoring and occasionally made somnolent yipping noises. There was something comforting about a sleeping dog curled up in your lap.

The dimly lit and humid room made me drowsy, and my head drooped toward my chest.

I heard the muffled sound of a conch shell being blown and felt myself being lifted out of my body. I turned back and saw myself sitting cross-legged on the floor of the yurt. Then my spirit body floated up, and I was amazed and delighted to be bobbing around effortlessly. I drifted out through the yurt roof and looked down to see the dark jungle beneath me. In the distance, I saw an array of flickering amber lights and willed myself to fly toward them. As I drew closer, I saw a shadowy processional of native warriors. Heading up the entourage was Lono in an ornate feathered headdress and a loin cloth, carrying a large, curved sword. As I bobbed above him, he looked up and acknowledged my presence with a curt nod. Then I was falling hard and fast like a heavy stone, plummeting back to Earth.

I jerked awake and found myself lying on my back inside the darkened yurt. The candles on the altar flickered and provided an ambient glow. My head rested on a round pillow, I was covered up with a cotton yoga blanket.

My head hurt, and I realized I hadn't eaten in a while. *Where is everyone?* I sat up, stretched, and wondered what happened. The chirping noise of the coqui frogs enveloped the yurt, and I found it oddly comforting to hear a familiar sound.

I got to my feet, folded the blanket, and put both it and pillow away near the altar, then stepped out into the cool night air and slipped on my flip flops. I wondered what time it was and how long I'd napped as I started back to the lodge, hoping Kailani was still awake.

***

The lodge was dark except for the bright motion sensor light above the main entrance. I looked over to the kitchen and saw lights on and heard the murmuring of soft voices. When I walked into the kitchen, Kailani and Diana were sitting at the long dining table, and I was greeted by Diana, who was shuffling a deck of tarot cards.

"Hey, sleepyhead!" she said. "We're having chai tea, would you like some?" Diana asked.

"I'd love some ice tea if there's any left. But I'm actually starved… is there anything to eat?"

"I saved a plate for you." Kailani got up and came back with a dinner plate of soba noodles dressed with sesame oil and bits of nori seaweed, a grilled tofu patty, and an avocado sushi roll. The food looked fresh and tasty. Yet what I really craved was a juicy double cheeseburger. She also put a glass of ice tea down in front of me.

"Thank you," I said. "So, what are the cards for?"

"Just for fun," Diana said. "Would you like a reading?"

"Sure… why not?"

Diana fanned out the tarot deck. "Pick a card."

I reached for a card in the middle of the spread.

Diana and Kailani leaned over. "You got the priestess card!" Diana said.

I peered at the image of a crow standing on a yellow crescent moon. A white veil surrounded its head.

"This card represents the divine feminine. It indicates tapping into your own inner wisdom and intuition."

"That's an unusual deck," I said.

"It was a birthday present from me!" Kailani said. "The veil symbolizes how this creature inhabits both worlds of material and spiritual."

"And this card suggests to see things how they really are… *not what we want them to be.*"

I handed the card back to Diana. They were both looking at me expectantly.

"So, what'd the ancestors have to say to you in the yurt?" Kailani asked.

"I'm not sure what it all means, but I saw Lono dressed as a warrior, leading a troop of men."

"*Night marchers!*" Diana said.

I looked at her and furrowed my brows. "What are you talking about?"

"There's a legend of dead warriors from the past roaming the island," Kailani explained.

"I saw them once," Diana added. "Well, actually, I *heard* them. I heard a conch shell being blown. Then I saw a column of men carrying torches. It was pretty vivid."

"You might have traveled back in time," Kailani said.

I picked up an avocado roll. "I'm not sure what to think."

Diana chuckled. "All kinds of strange things happen around here. I've seen water spirits churning the ocean at night. Remember that, Kailani?"

Kailani nodded. "We were facilitating a women's retreat at the beach at night. Diana and I drove them out to Secret Beach for a moonlight meditation. They had their own ceremony planned, we were just dropping them off. We went back an hour later to check on them and they were in this deep trance. I don't know what they were doing, but the ocean started churning."

"Kailani and I look up, and there's this gigantic wave rolling toward the shore, right at us," Diana said. "It was surreal. Then the wind started to pick up. I knew we had to get the hell out of there!"

"We had to shake those women awake, get them going. I was dragging two of them by their arms," Kailani added.

"I managed to get the last three awake, and I literally pushed them through the jungle toward the van," Diana said.

"After we got back here, I told them to never do that again. They were trying to summon Pele's, sister *Namaka*, the goddess of the sea," Kailani said.

"People don't understand how powerful the forces are out here!" Diana said. "If we hadn't gone back to check on them, they would have been washed away!"

"Why would I dream about Lono being a night marcher?"

"Dreams sometimes represent something in our inner world. Lono could represent your inner warrior—being fierce and brave?" Kailani said.

"It took courage to leave your marriage," Diana added. "You left with nothing."

"Or the ancestors are showing you what a real man is supposed to be. Someone with honor, integrity, and is willing to sacrifice and protect for the community."

Traits that Jason didn't exactly exemplify.

***

Kailani, Diana, and I finished our night enjoying a vegan mango cheesecake with a nutty crust that Kailani had made. I decided to bring a piece to Cassie over at the lodge. After we said our goodnights, I put a piece in a Tupperware container and headed over.

The coqui frogs seemed less loud over at the lodge. I entered through the front doors and went down a short hallway to Cassie's room, where I rapped lightly on the door. Cassie flung the door open wearing a pale-blue, fuzzy, chenille bathrobe with white daisy appliques at the hem. Her hair was wet.

"Hey, what's up?" she asked and gestured for me to come in.

"I brought you some dessert... mango cheesecake." I handed her the Tupperware.

Cassie took it and looked at it suspiciously. "Is it really cheesecake or is it fake cheese?"

"It's *vegan*... so not real dairy. But it's pretty good."

"I'd kill for a steak right now," Cassie sighed. "And some onion rings!"

"We could go into Hilo tomorrow and get some Philly cheese steak sandwiches."

Cassie put the Tupperware down on a wood dresser facing the king sized bed. The room was tastefully decorated in shades of cream, gold, and light green, the king sized bed boasting cream-colored chenille comforter with pale green pillows.

"It's cozy in here," I said.

Cassie stretched out on the bed while I plopped down on the gold loveseat. "These sheets are so soft."

"They're probably bamboo. Kailani told me they only have organic cotton or bamboo sheets. They avoid synthetics because of the micro plastic pollution in the air and the water. They've even found fibers in the Arctic!"

Cassie sighed. "I avoid synthetics in general. No polyester for this girl, so I'm doing my bit for the environment. I even drive a Tesla."

I made no comment about that, since the lithium batteries caused all kinds of pollution with the heavy mining of cobalt, so I kept my mouth shut.

"So, what happened to you? You, like, *passed out*," Cassie said.

"I don't know. I had a really weird dream about Lono."

I described the dream to Cassie, who listened intently.

"You know, when we were kids, you were just like Kai," Cassie said. She opened her eyes and looked at me. "You guys would talk about fairies and stuff. I always thought that's why you guys were so tight."

"*Really*? I don't remember that at all."

"One time, you said your Aunt Lily punished you for making up stories about fairies and elves!"

"I remember that. She banned me from watching TV for a whole week."

"So, you do remember!"

"I remember getting punished and missing the TV show *M.A.S.H* for a week. Aunt Lily was no-nonsense and strict. She'd get upset when I mentioned anything supernatural. There was another time when I told her I could see people's aura and she freaked out. Told me to never talk about it."

"Your aunt meant well, but she was a nervous Nellie." Cassie got up and went to the wooden dresser, opened the top drawer, and pulled out a blue box of chocolate covered macadamia nuts. "Have some."

"I guess you're not eating the vegan cheesecake then?"

"*Hell no!*"

With that, Cassie enthusiastically popped a chocolate into her mouth with a grin.

***

I left Cassie's room and started back to my cabin. I'd heard a few drops of rain splatter on the window and decided to scoot before a downpour hit.

I passed the darkened kitchen, and in minutes, I was at my cabin. It was good timing, as there was a dramatic flash of lightning that lit up the grassy meadow in front of the cabin. A loud clap of thunder soon followed, and I darted inside before a heavy torrent of rain pummeled my dwelling.

It took me a while to fall asleep. The rain lashed noisily against the cabin windows and tin roof. I even put a pillow over my head hoping to muffle the noise. When I finally dozed, I dreamt about Lono, walking through the jungle with a big white dog. He was wearing the feathered warrior head dress. They both turned to look at me, and the dog barked fiercely at me.

A noise at my front door jerked me awake, and I sat up in bed, realizing it was a dog barking. For a disoriented moment, I nervously worried if there was a big white dog on the doorstep. Then I heard a dainty scratching noise and a faint dog whimper. I cracked the door open slightly and saw Ozzie peering up at me. When I opened it wider, he charged in and launched himself on my bed.

"*Hey!*" I protested.

I grabbed a beach towel hanging off a chair and scooped him up, wrapped him like a doggy burrito.

"You are soaking wet. What are you doing here, Ozzie?"

He wriggled around, making cute canine noises. I put him down on the floor and he looked up at the bed again.

"Okay, hang on." I draped the towel over the comforter as Ozzie relaunched himself onto the bed. "Kailani isn't going to be happy about you running amok!" I said.

Ozzie opened his mouth wide in a comical yawn. It was obvious he was the lord of the manor.

Chapter Fifteen

I awoke feeling a dampness between my legs. I got out of bed and pulled down my pajama shorts to find dark blood stains. I hadn't had a menstrual cycle in months. Murphy's Law, the pajamas were a brand new flowered Kate Spade set I'd splurged on while shopping with Cassie at Nordstroms. Normally, I was content with an oversized Gap sleepshirt. However, as I watched Cassie drop five hundred dollars on Felina bras, I'd decided to indulge in something pretty.

I went over to the closet and pulled out my overnight bag, hoping there might be an old tampon hidden somewhere. relieved to find a crumpled, sealed pantyliner. I changed into a pair of clean panties, then had to head over to the outdoor communal bath house to rinse the blood out.

Luckily, the retreat center had emptied out for the day, so I'd have the bathhouse to myself. The Japanese honeymooners had checked out the day before. Last night, I'd been invited to join Diana, Lono, and Cassie to pick up supplies for the next influx of guests. I had begged off since I enjoyed sleeping in and having the bathhouse to myself. I threw on my cotton kimono robe and flip flops and headed over to the bathhouse. Outside, there was a cool, dewy freshness to the air. The sky was a translucent turquoise blue, with a few puffy, cream clouds.

The bathhouse smelled faintly of lavender thanks to the homemade cleaning spray that Kailani used. I turned on the cold water faucet and rinsed out the short, the blood swirling around the white porcelain sink, and an unhappy childhood memory surfaced.

I had been eleven years old at school when I got my first period. Luckily, it was lunch hour, and I raced into the lavatory thinking I'd wet my pants. To my shock, my panties were soaked with blood. I stuffed toilet paper in the crotch to absorb the blood and found my way to the school nurse's office in shock. I was sure the nurse would help me.

Nurse Luci was a calming presence. She reassured me that I was fine and discreetly took out a small cardboard box from her desk drawer. The box contained a sanitary napkin

Most of the blood washed away, and as I started to wring the shorts out, Kailani burst into the bathhouse carrying a mop and bucket.

"Sorry!" she said.

"You're good, but I can't say the same for my new pajamas,"

I held the wet bottoms up to show her. "Can you believe it… brand new Kate Spade and I got my period."

"You're still getting periods?"

"I haven't for months. Do you have any tampons or pantyliners?"

"Back in our cabin. Come on."

She set the mop and bucket outside and we walked toward the lodge together.

"Do you remember Nurse Luci? I had this funny flashback to when I got my first period. She gave me my first feminine pad."

"Nurse Luci…wow. I haven't thought of her in years. She was always so nice."

"It was lucky that she was around. When I told Aunt Lily later, she freaked out."

"She did? *Why?*"

I shrugged. "At first she didn't believe me—said I was too young. Then Nurse Luci called to check up on me, and she got more upset. She said I shouldn't have confided in a stranger."

Kailani shook her head. "Wow. I had the opposite experience. *Tutu* hugged me and we celebrated with custard tarts from Chinatown. She told me how indigenous women celebrated their moon cycles by gathering in a lodge to bask in the strong feminine energies."

"I'd heard that too, but the version I heard was that women were kept away from the men during the cycles. Probably for the mens protection with PMS and all," I joked.

Kailani laughed. "So much has been misrepresented over time, hasn't it?" As we walked past the kitchen, she suggested, "Why don't you relax with some tea, and I'll bring the tampons to you. Our place is a mess."

"Sure, no problem."

I went into the kitchen to find Ozzie dozing on his puffy, round, dog bed. He opened one eye and went back to snoozing.

"It's a dog's life here!"

He didn't respond to my remark. I went to the refrigerator, took out a pitcher of tropical ice tea, found two juice glasses in the sink, and poured one for Kailani as well. A few minutes later, she re-appeared with a box of pantyliners.

"Here you go—sorry, that's all we have."

She put the box on the long dining table, and I handed her a glass of ice tea.

"Thanks, but I have so much to do before the next guests get here."

"You're always reminding me to take time to smell the roses. So, here you go. Take a breather."

"You're right. Lets go out and sit outside."

We took our ice teas and flopped down on a wicker loveseat on the patio. Kailani reached over and patted my arm.

"I had no idea your Aunt Lily was so uptight. That must have been tough, especially since your first moon time is so special."

Her tender words brought tears to my eyes. I hadn't mentioned the experience to anyone, and hearing her articulate what I felt all those years ago was painful. I quickly brushed away the tears with the back of my hand.

"Thank God for Nurse Luci. She gave me my first Moddess sanitary napkin in a box. Remember those… pre-tampons?"

"Oh my God… *yes!* And the sanitary napkin elastic belt. Ugh… talk about awkward!"

We both chuckled. I hadn't realized how much I missed spending quality time with Kailani just hanging out. The past few years felt like there were always distractions with spouses, children, animals, and work. Our visits became brief, rushed interludes spent catching up but not really connecting.

"I'm so envious of the life you and Shara built together."

"You had it with Jason in the beginning. I know he made you feel safe and secure. It's hard to let that go, I get it."

I didn't think Kailani really did get it. I always envied her cozy family unit—her doting grandmother and all her cousins. We had bonded over the fact that we were brown girls with divorced parents being raised by relatives on the mainland.

"I kept wishing your grandmother would adopt me!"

"We *did* adopt you! You're family… me, you, and *Tutu*. You *belong.*"

New tears filled my eyes at her loving words.

"Awww, sweetie… shhhhhh." Kailani put her arm around my shoulders and squeezed.

"I still dream about the pink bakery boxes she'd bring over filled with fresh doughnuts!"

"Tutu always made sure to get extra maple glazed old fashioneds because she knew they were your favorite."

I sat up and looked at Kailani. "Cassie reminded me that we used to play with fairies at night. Do you remember that?"

She chuckled. "I still play with fairies here on the island. They're all around us. You just have to tune in. Shara's kids always tell us how the nature devas talk to them. When we were children, it was so easy because adults indulged in our make believe stories. Then we grew up and it wasn't socially acceptable to talk about that stuff."

"And we get caught up in our day-to-day lives, trying to make money and make our spouses happy."

She nodded. "Unfortunately true. We stopped believing in magic. You know, you could come live here. We need a part-time office manager to keep us organized. What do you think? Rodrigo would love it here!"

The offer was tantalizing. I briefly imagined Rodrigo and I living in paradise happily ever after. He could easily get work.

"I dreamt about him last night. At least I think I dreamt about him—it seemed so real. I woke up and I could feel him lying next to me, caressing my hair and nuzzling my neck!"

"Have you talked to him lately?"

I shook my head. "With the three hour time difference, we keep missing each other. He's either at work or asleep it seems."

"You know, when souls are as deeply connected as you two, it doesn't surprise me that he'd visit you in the astral realm."

"I miss him. I keep thinking I should invite him to come visit."

"Why don't you?"

I sighed. "I've kept him at arm's length because I was sorting out Jason and me. I don't want to lead him on when I'm not sure what I want."

"He's a big boy. A very handsome big boy!"

"You think so?" Her comment surprised me.

"Just because I love women doesn't mean I don't notice a good looking man."

"He's so much younger than me. He says he doesn't want kids, but what if he changes his mind later?"

"Like I said, he's a big boy, and if he changes his mind, so what? You want happily ever after, but you know there's no guarantees. You have to be happy and feel thankful right this moment. Tutu used to give thanks every day for the sun rising. I thought that was weird. But then there was that time about eighteen years ago when we had no sun for forty days. We take things for granted. What are you thankful for?"

"I'm thankful to be here with you. I'm thankful we all reconnected. I'm thankful we're going dancing at Uncle Roberts tonight!"

I heard a sharp bark, and we both turned and saw Ozzie alert and panting with his pink tongue hanging out.

"And this one is thankful for his endless supply of dog treats!"

Ozzie barked again. His eyes were bright, and you I see the mischief lurking there.

***

Uncle Robert's was the community live music venue for locals on Wednesday nights. Kailani pulled up and dropped us off while she parked. Cassie, Diana, and I hopped out, and immediately the strong odor of marijuana smoke filled my nostrils. Diana wrinkled her nose but laughed.

"Definitely a 420 friendly place," she joked.

It was a festive scene, with food booths hawking tasty food and local residents mingling and laughing. As we made our way through the noisy crowd, I heard the local band doing a cover of Clarence Clearwater's song "Up Around the Bend." Cassie was already near the stage, swaying to the music. She waved Diana and me over with a big grin. Diana waved back but headed toward a food booth while I wended my way toward the stage.

"Hey, beautiful."

I turned to see a man with a huge lionhead mask, complete with flowing, golden-brown mane and glassy amber eyes. He wore a pale blue Hawaiian print shirt with postcard sized images of Elvis in his white jumpsuit over beige cargo shorts and black flip flops.

"Would you like to dance?" he asked.

"Sure,"

He slipped his arm around my waist and clasped his hand with mine. He held me close as we swayed in a clumsy two step to the music, and a strange tingling sensation coursed over my body, goosebumps fanning down both my arms.

"Are you having a good time?" he asked.

"Uncle Robert's is always fun."

He twirled me around and drew me in even closer. I noticed that Cassie was dancing with a man in a green, knitted octopus head, the octopus arms swayed to the music as they shimmied together. Even stranger was someone wearing a big, plastic, green dinosaur costume, spinning around near the stage alone. The *anything goes* vibe at Uncle Robert's was always surreal, but tonight seemed to exist on a new level of strangeness.

I started feeling dizzy and overwhelmed from the loud music and the pot cloud that hung over the venue. The song changed from "Up Around the Bend" to Elvis's "Suspicious Minds."

"Are you with anyone tonight?" Lion Man asked.

"My girlfriends,"

I nodded toward Cassie. "She seems to be enjoying the octo man,"

Something about the Lion Man seemed familiar. My scalp prickled with nervousness. *Who is he?* I had a fleeting suspicion that Lion Man was Jason. His voice was muffled through the mask, so I couldn't be sure.

"Would you like to come back to my lair tonight?" he teased.

"I don't hook up with lions I don't know."

As I said this, a heat simmered below my waist. I even had a crazy, fleeting desire to go off with him and throw caution to the wind.

He chuckled. "You could get to know me."

"You're pretty sure of yourself."

"I'm the king of the jungle. I'm looking for my lioness."

An uncomfortable twitch fluttered in my stomach. *Danger!*

The Lion Man pressed me closer. "I'll be whoever you want," he said.

There was something silky and compelling about his voice. I was both turned on and discomfited. I abruptly pulled away from Lion Man as a familiar voice surprised me from behind.

"Mind if I cut in, *brah*?"

I turned to see Lono beside me. He took my hand and led me away. Lion Man called out, "I'll see you again."

"You okay?" Lono asked.

He smiled down at me as he took both my hands and held them as we swayed to the music.

"Thanks for cutting in."

"You seemed like you were in distress."

"I know it sounds crazy, but for a split second, I was sure it was Jason."

"Maybe it was."

"Is that what you think?"

"What did you *sense?*"

"There was something familiar about him. It made me uncomfortable."

"Perhaps that familiarity was the energy signature of your former husband."

"I'm not sure what you mean?"

"You and Kailani are empaths… you sense things that most people have no awareness of. Kailani's abilities have been amplified since she moved back. I believe that's why the ancestors summoned you here."

"For what purpose?"

"So you can discover your true self. The ancestors speak to you in symbols that get your attention. You see crows and butterflies while you sleep and in your waking state. They symbolize something. Do you know what that is?" He leaned in close and gazed intently into my eyes. A pleasant rippling sensation swept throughout my body. It wasn't sexual, but it felt like the cells in my body were vibrating.

"What does the crow mean to you?"

I shook my head. "I'm not sure. I know in indigenous cultures, the crow has a mystical meaning, as in transformation."

"There you go. Don't you think you're in a space of transformation now?"

"I'd say I'm more in a limbo state."

"Maybe you can reframe that. The Chinese *I Ching* danger hexagram counsels to stay true to yourself with integrity and honesty during perilous times. It also counsels to stay in rest and shore up your inner strength. Tell me, do you think your ex-husband is a man of honor?"

His eyes locked onto mine intently, the question startling me and I didn't know how to respond.

"Wouldn't an honorable man fulfill his obligations on time?"

My face went hot. "Jason was going through a lot. He paid me back eventually,'"

Why was I being so defensive?

"So, you are saying he is a man of honor?"

I didn't know how to respond.

"How about something to drink?" Lono suggested.

"I'm not thirsty, but I could use a bite to eat," I said.

Lono put his arm around my waist and propelled me toward the parking lot.

"Where are we going? What about the others?"

"They'll be fine."

He helped me into his truck, got in, and started the engine. As he pulled out, I turned to see Lion Man in his Elvis shirt walking out. As Lono backed the truck out, Lion Man removed his mask, and our eyes locked. It was Jason.

***

"Why didn't I know it was Jason?" I sighed.

"You *did know*. You said you sensed his energy."

151

I recalled how I was both attracted and put off at the same time. My body desired to rendezvous with him, but a stronger force stopped me.

"It was the lionhead and the pot smoke. It disoriented me."

We were eating burgers at the Burger Joint, and I was stuffing French fries in my mouth that were sinfully good. I took a bite out of my California burger and savored the avocado and bacon yummy mouth feel. Lono had the fish burger. I took a healthy swig of my diet Coke.

"Noelani… you did know. You *sensed* him."

I stuffed more French fries into my mouth. The salty crispiness made me want to swoon. "I even thought about going with him. I felt this weird magnetic pull."

"You *see*?"

Lono sipped his beer. The burger place was surprisingly bustling, even though it was almost closing time. The long, dark, wooden bar was lined with chatty customers. It seemed like a popular local watering hole.

"You knew right away," I said.

"I did. That's why I thought we should leave."

"Did the ancestors warn you?"

He nodded with a smile and pushed his plate toward me. He'd barely touched his fries.

"You've been eyeballing them. I'm full," Lono said.

"You think Jason will try to come out to Kailani's?"

Lono took in a long breath. "*No.* The ancestors won't permit it."

"But they allowed him to get this close to me? That doesn't make sense."

"Maybe they were testing you… to see what you would do?"

"In that case, I almost failed. I wanted to go home with him."

"But you didn't. Why?"

"It felt wrong. It was like a forcefield popped up to prevent me. It was a weird feeling."

I had always allowed Jason to dominate me in many ways—especially in bed. I felt it was my wifely duty to submit to him when he wanted, even though I wasn't always in the mood, and the post-coital tenderness had been non-existent at the end. I thought about Rodrigo's loving caresses and how he always stayed with me instead of abruptly leaving.

"You followed your instincts. I'm proud of you. You honored yourself."

A pleasant warmth fanned through my body at Lono's kind words. The unresolved heaviness that had weighed me down for months seemed to magically disperse in the spirited laughter around me. *Maybe a piece of me has finally come home to the islands.*

Chapter Sixteen

I sat cross-legged on top of the bed, writing in my butterfly diary. *"I dreamt I was dancing with the Lion Man. He ripped off his lion's head, and it was Jason. We kissed passionately, but when I opened my eyes, his face had become disfigured. Ugly, jagged scars lined his face, and his mouth was twisted grotesquely. I backed away, and then suddenly he turned into my high school boyfriend Declan. I was confused. Declan took my hand and led me to a graveyard. Swirling gray mists of fog obscured my vision as we walked past headstones, A black snake sprang up from the ground, hissing and lunging at my legs. I staggered away fearfully. Declan leaned over and picked up the snake. "Trust," he whispered. Then his face dissolved, and I was staring into Lono's dark eyes, and I saw galaxies of brilliant stars swirling inside his pupils."*

Three different men representing three different aspects. Jason's distorted visage showed me the ugliness under the mask. Declan represented the sweet innocence of our teenage love and how I could always count on him. Finally, Lono, who represented infinite possibilities and also another man I could trust. I was evolving and realized how losing the restaurant had caused Jason to *devolve*. How his identity was wrapped up in being a successful restaurateur and I was just an accoutrement. I had willingly played the pseudo trophy wife by always dressing up for him. My hair and make-up were perfect not because I liked to but because it was important to him that I looked a certain way.

There was a knock at my cabin door, and I put my diary down on the bed and opened it to find Cassie standing in front of me. She was dressed in a bright-pink and peach plumeria maxi dress with a straw hat.

"You've gone native!" I joked.

"I wanted to say goodbye before I took off," Cassie said.

"You're going back to California already?"

Cassie gestured inside the cabin, so I stepped aside to let her in, where she sank down on the edge of the bed, and I sat down beside her.

"I'm meeting Steve on Maui. We talked for a while last night, and I told him I was pregnant. He's flying in today."

My arms rippled with goosebumps. *They're getting back together!*

"But… you finally got divorced," I said.

Cassie threw her hands up. "*I know!* He got all emotional, and then we both started crying. God… what a mess. Maybe it's a sign that I got knocked up—like the universe is giving us a second chance."

"You don't even know if you're actually pregnant. What if it's a false positive?"

"It's not. I went to an urgent care clinic yesterday and got tested."

"So, you're running back to Steve just because Montrell dumped you!" My voice sounded harsher and more shrill than I intended.

"You're jealous because Steve is stepping up for me and my baby. You can't face the fact that Jason cared more about that damn restaurant than you!"

My face went hot with anger. "You have no idea what you're talking about."

"Jason was cheating on you with Candace. I know because Blake told me!"

My body went cold. "What are you talking about?"

"The last time you and I had lunch, I bumped into Blake at the bar when I got to the restaurant. He was already pretty shitfaced and badmouthing Jason and Candace. They hadn't even told him they'd sold the place. He said it was bad enough Jason guilted you into loaning him the money but that Jason and Candace were a *thing* for the past year. The whole staff knew."

Jason and Candace... all those nights he didn't come home. He'd said he slept on the sofa in his office. I couldn't breathe, and a clamminess spread all over my body. Cassie's pitying look was all I could take. I heard a loud thump against the cabin window and looked up to see a black crow frantically pecking on the glass. *As if things couldn't get weirder.*

"I'm sorry, Noelani. I should have told you, but Kailani said not to."

A cheating husband is one type of betrayal. A loyal friend that withholds secrets is another type of betrayal—it hurt *more*.

"You should leave," I choked out. My throat tightened, and I crossed my arms over my chest. The room felt like it was spinning. Cassie got up quietly and went to the door. She started to say something else but stopped, then left and closed the door.

***

Kailani was busy on her laptop in the kitchen. She sat perched on a high bar stool with her reading glasses on as she peered at the computer screen.

"So, you and Cassie knew about Jason's affair!"

Kailani stood and put her hands up as if to ward off my angry accusation.

"Don't be angry at Cassie—this is on me. I was trying to protect you. *I'm sorry.*"

She got off the stool and took a step toward me. I backed away.

"I need to be alone," I blurted.

I hurried out of the kitchen and stomped furiously down the gravel driveway toward the main road. Hot tears spilled down my face, and I brushed them away with the back of my hand.

Why was it my fate to be alone and abandoned by everyone close to me? First my own mother, who promised to come for me, then various lovers, and then my former husband. *But now Kailani?* I saw the turnout to Turtle Beach ahead and stumbled into the parking lot.

There was a weathered wooden bench surrounded by a thick copse of leafy, green mango trees. I sank down heavily on the weathered wooden bench with my shoulders hunched, gripping the edges of the bench, and stared down at my feet, trying to will away the dark hopelessness that washed over me.

A few tourists milled around, taking photos of the rugged coastline below. Here was another contradiction in my life—living in a tropical paradise, feeling wretched while others were busy enjoying the limpid ocean water and perfect sun-soaked beaches.

I heard a flutter of beating wings and looked up to see a crow perched on a mango tree branch over my head.

"You again!" I said.

He cocked his head to one side and silently observed me.

"Leave me alone."

His answer was to fly straight at me and furiously dive bomb my head. The wings batted at my face, then a few rapid, sharp pecks on my scalp. *What the hell?* I swatted frantically at him. He nimbly flew away and hopped back on the branch.

Someone whispered the word *time to let go!* I looked around, but there was no one near me except for the beady-eyed crow. Harsh, self-punishing thoughts flooded my mind. *How could I have been so gullible? Why had I put up with Jason's selfish behavior all that time? Because I was a people pleaser. Because I thought he was my soulmate and I had to sacrifice to make him happy. Because I was a doormat.* The crow let out a loud *caw. Great! Is this what my life is reduced to... being randomly stalked by menacing crows?*

"Hey."

I looked up to see Kailani standing behind me. She waved a stainless steel thermos at me.

"Peace offering? I brought some ice tea," she said with a contrite smile. "Can I sit down?"

I nodded. She unscrewed the top of the thermos and offered it to me. I took a sip. The sweetened tea was refreshing.

"How are you doing?"

"*Awful.* I'm just beating myself up for being a doormat."

"You weren't a doormat. One of the things I love about you is your tender heart."

I let out a bitter laugh. "That night we slept together—he swore nothing was going on between him and Candace. Then he got that sext message from her. *God!*"

"I'm so sorry."

"I remember one huge fight we had. He invited some investors over to the restaurant to impress them. He wanted me to be there and look pretty. I didn't want to go because I was having massive cramps. I was bloated and gross and I wanted to stay home with my heating pad. I told him I wasn't feeling well, and he got so angry. He accused me of not being supportive—that this meeting could mean a lot of money and that the restaurant needed major repairs to stay afloat. So, I compromised, I said I'd go for a little while. I was miserable the whole time. I put on a fake smiley face and pretended everything was okay."

"Did he get the money?"

I nodded. "He plied them with free booze, and they all got drunk and stupid. Candace was there too, and she sucked up to them big time. At one point, I told them I had to go to the ladies' room and slipped away. Jason didn't even notice. I asked him the next day how things went, and he never mentioned me being missing!"

"Did he even thank you for showing up?"

I shook my head. "The worst part was having to sell the townhouse to pay off the restaurant debts toward the end. Remember how we remodeled the whole kitchen? It was my dream kitchen—I picked every tile for the countertops."

A jab of grief flooded me as I recalled the beautiful, cobalt-blue tiled kitchen counters with the complementary, yellow backsplash border. Even the matching ceramic sink had a unique design. I even missed the pull-down, brass, gooseneck faucet. I sighed and brushed fresh tears away.

Kailani put her hand on my knee and squeezed. "It was a beautiful kitchen."

"Everyone gets to have a *happily ever after* except me. Even you and Shara have a perfect life."

Kailani sighed. "We have our issues too. It's not easy being a stepmother to three kids. They're good kids, but they miss their father and being on the continent. He's behind on child support payments, and Shara is at her wit's end. Not to mention Shara's mother is battling dementia. She might have to come live with us. We can't afford to pay for a nursing home."

Listening to Kailani's travails made me thankful I didn't have to deal with a deadbeat former husband or a seriously ill parent. My problems were so trivial in comparison.

"I'm sorry you two are going through that. I have nothing to complain about."

Kailani waved her hand dismissively. "Look, Jason was your world for twenty years. You two had a wonderful life together. He gave you a home and a sense of belonging. He made you feel special. You never had that before. It's not easy to give that up."

"You're right. He always had a knack of making me feel special. I remember the first time I spent the night at his place, he made me a bubble bath with fresh rose petals, scented candles, and even bought new towels."

"I remember you telling me that."

"I guess I thought he'd fight for me… for *us*. Instead, he just got lost in drinking too much and numbing out. Now, he's probably pampering Candace with bubble baths."

"Don't *go there*. You're better off without him. I mean, do you really want to be with someone who lied to your face?"

"Lono said Jason had no honor."

Kailani squeezed my knee sympathetically.

"I had a strange dream last night about Jason." I described the dream to her, mulling over my interpretation. "It reminded me of that time we saw Phantom of the Opera. Remember the phantom's hideous face? That's what Jason looked like."

"What do you think it means?"

"I'm not sure. Maybe my dream was telling me that… I'm seeing his true face. But that part about Lono's eyes." I shivered.

"Lono is definitely a mystery. Even growing up together, I couldn't figure him out—he always kept to himself. You know what's really weird… he only sleeps four hours a day. Isn't that crazy. I turn into a shrieking banshee with less than eight hours!"

"There is an otherworldly quality about him. Sometimes the funny way he looks at me, I feel he's about to let me in on a secret," I said.

"He used to worry his family because he said he could hear the night marchers. He'd describe the conch shell sound and claim he could hear soldiers walking past the house. Nothing surprises me about my cousin anymore. Aren't you guys going turtle watching tomorrow?"

I nodded.

"Don't overthink things… try to enjoy your precious time on the island," she urged.

"I wish you'd move back to California so we could hang out again."

"We really do need your help organizing our office. We can't pay a lot, but you'd get your own cabin. Think of it as a fresh start."

I rested my head on Kailani's shoulder and breathed in the salty air. A cool, caressing breeze soothed my heated skin. *A fresh start.* It was an idea that was growing on me.

Chapter Seventeen

"Here we are," Lono said. As always, he looked confident and handsome, dressed casually in his black San Francisco Giant's t-shirt and matching black ball cap. His eyes were shaded by his usual black Ray-Ban sunglasses. It was a crime to look that good after only sleeping four hours.

I was back at Turtle Beach. It was hard to believe just twenty four hours ago, I had been an emotional wreck, but something had shifted in me.

I looked down the rocky cliffside at the blue-gray waves crashing wildly over craggy black rocks, leaving frothy white foam on the small beach. The sand looked like onyx gravel compared to the fine, golden, sandy beaches on Oahu. There was a desolate moonscape feel. A clamminess permeated over my skin, and I took a big step away from the cliff's edge, my heart thudding loudly in my ears.

"How are we supposed to get down there?"

Lono smiled with amusement. "By walking."

I looked down at the rough, single track trail lined with jagged, porous, volcanic black rocks. Clusters of lush green ferns clumped around the sides.

"I can't do this."

"Sure you can." He held his hand out to me.

"I'm serious. I'm not in great shape, and that is a long way to fall!"

Lono gripped my hand and gently tugged. "You've got this."

He took small, mincing backward steps as he led me down the narrow trail. My hiking sandals felt inadequate, and I couldn't believe he was wearing regular running shoes.

"Look at me. *Breathe!*" Lono said.

About halfway down the trail, I slipped on some pebbles and fell hard on my butt, feeling defeated and embarrassed.

Lono was immediately standing over me. "You okay?"

"I want to go back up, this is too much!" I moaned. The bottoms of my feet were sweaty and slippery in my sandals.

"Just a little bit further. You wanted to see turtles, right? Let's take a breather." Lono squatted down next to me, reached into his knapsack, pulled out an aluminum flask of water, and handed it to me.

I took a dainty sip, glancing down at the narrow beach as loud, white-tipped waves battered the stony outcropping. I had a paranoid vision of me plummeting over the cliff and being swallowed up by the churning foamy waters.

We sat in silence for a few minutes, and then Lono stood. "Come on, we're almost there. Keep your eyes on *me*. Don't look over the edge."

I got up reluctantly. My butt was throbbing from the fall, and I was self-conscious about being out of shape. So much for all those gym workout classes. We started up again, and it seemed to go quicker as the trail became less steep and I was more comfortable navigating the uneven, slippery ground. I gripped Lono's surprisingly strong hands as we proceeded in halting, small steps. When we landed on the actual beach, I noticed dried palm fronds and small tree branches littered the coarse, black sand.

The beach was eerily deserted, and there was an ominous gloom that permeated the bleak terrain. Lono had kicked off his running shoes and pulled a beach towel from his knapsack, which he spread on the ground. I plopped down beside him.

"People have drowned here," I said. "I can feel it."

"The undertow here is quite strong. You have to be in good shape and a strong swimmer. I have heard the sirens of the ocean calling to me. Their voices are seductive."

"You must be a strong swimmer then!"

Lono ducked his head, avoiding my gaze. "My body was made to withstand the waves."

The roar of the dramatic waves filled my ears, and I looked up at the rugged cliff face that we had just trudged down. My stomach clenched when I realized we had to go back up eventually.

"Come on, let's take a dip!" Lono had taken off his cotton t-shirt and ball cap and looked down at me expectantly. He stuck his hand out once more.

"No way," I replied. "I've had enough excitement for one day."

"Just stick your feet in then."

How could I resist that roguish smile? I found myself staring at his perfectly shaped, ivory, white teeth against a bronze, oval face.

"Okay, fine."

He pulled me to my feet and held my hand as we moved over to the water's edge.

"Look at that wave!" Lono said.

As I tilted my head up, I was stunned to see a mammoth wave, at least three stories high, curling toward us. I instinctively scrambled backward, but Lono grabbed my wrist, and I looked up into his eyes and saw the spiraling stars from my dream. *What the hell?*

"Trust me, Noelani. Hop onto my back."

"*Lono!*" I stammered. "*I can't do this. Please!*"

"*Trust me, sista, now!*"

Something in his eyes ignited me into action, and I quickly hopped onto his back, my legs clamped onto his waist and my arms locked around his neck and shoulders. The thunderous roar of the wave surrounded us as Lono leapt into the water, and for a brief, crazy moment, we were floating above the water. I screamed, and then I was violently drenched in saltwater. I coughed as the briny water burned my throat and nose. My eyes were squeezed shut and I prayed fervently that we'd survive.

"*Lono,*" I sputtered.

To my shock, we were gliding effortlessly through the water. It was the oddest sensation of sluicing through the waves. We gradually slowed down and floated on top of the water.

My muscles loosened, and a peace rippled through me. I opened my eyes and was shocked to see that *Lono had turned into a giant sea turtle!* I gasped. He turned to look at me, and I was staring into a pointed, mottled, amphibian face with dark, liquid eyes.

Oh my God. I wasn't touching soft human skin, I was holding onto a hard shell. His smooth arms had become hard, tapered flippers. My legs rested against his hard shell.

"Relax," Lono soothed. *"You're fine… we're fine."*

The words popped telepathically in my head.

I prayed I was dreaming and I'd soon wake up and find myself on the beach with Lono next to me—looking normal. Before I had a chance to process what was happening, a priestess seal popped up alongside us. Its sleek, dark head and whiskered face was inches from mine.

The seal transmitted a thought to me, *"Welcome, friend."*

All three of us floated in place briefly, then the seal swiftly darted under the water. *I have to be dreaming!* I heard more splashing sounds and saw two silvery flashes as a pair of spinner dolphins sped past us. As scared as I was, there was a part of me that thought I was having a really awesome hallucination. It was definitely going to make a hell of an entry in my diary.

***

The comforting rays of the sun warmed my face as my eyes fluttered open, and I sat up slowly and looked around. There was no sign of Lono, and a jab of fear pulsed through me. My mouth was still briny from swallowing seawater. I was also naked except for my damp panties. I saw my tank top and denim cutoffs drying on a nearby rock, then spotted Lono perched on a boulder down the beach. He stared tacitly over the ocean, and I sensed a melancholy about him. I got up and moved over to where he was sitting.

"Hey," I said.

"Hey yourself," he joked.

Somehow I didn't feel self-conscious despite the fact my breasts were exposed and my wet panties clung to my crotch. I put a hand on his shoulder.

"You want to be there… *with them.*"

"I belong to two worlds, but I can't fully inhabit either." His voice was wistful.

"It must get lonely."

He nodded.

"I have so many questions!" I blurted.

"*Ask.*"

"You said before that you almost drowned once and the turtles saved you. Why didn't you just transform?"

"I was pretty drunk. I can't just hit the water and become turtle man," he joked. "I have to float in the water, merge with the ocean, and consciously choose to transform."

For some weird reason, this made sense to me.

"When did you discover that you were different? Kailani told me that you used to swim with turtles as a child."

"I think I was maybe five or so when I transformed the first time. My *tutu* saw it happen, but she'd had a premonition about me. She was a gifted healer and had many medicine dreams. She said the ancestors whispered the words *turtle boy* when I was born. My own mother didn't know… only *tutu.* My mother didn't believe in the ancestors. My father had insisted she renounce any native beliefs after they got married. He was very devout and devoted to his church."

"Sorry."

He shrugged. "She was determined to be a devout wife, and her life was devoted to his religion. She tried to be a good mother."

Something in the way he said it made me think of Aunt Lily. She'd tried to be a good mother to me but wasn't accepting of my paranormal proclivities.

He asked, "When we got here, you said you sensed deaths here. What exactly did you feel?"

I shook my head in bewilderment. "There was a sense of despair."

I closed my eyes, and a vision formed of a limp body washed up on the beach. I described the scene to Lono.

"Do you see anything else?"

"There are people standing over the man. He seems older, with long gray hair and a beard. There's a shark's tooth on a brown leather cord around his neck. His name was… *Anthony?*"

Lono smiled. "How did you know this?"

I shrugged. "I just tuned into the energy of the beach."

"His name *was* Anthony. He lived nearby and used to body surf here regularly. Unfortunately, he had a weak heart."

"Then… why was he even swimming here? It seems risky."

"He loved it here. It was the way he chose to die."

That was a sobering thought.

"You want to try something?" Lono asked.

"Like *what*?"

"Let's get back in the water. I want to try an experiment."

"I'm not going to try to swim and end up like Anthony. I know my limitations!"

He laughed. "No, this will be fun. Come on."

I got up and followed Lono back to the water. Surprisingly, the ocean had calmed down. He went into the waves and held his arms out to me. I walked toward him, and he pulled me into his arms, the buoyancy of the water lifting me up. My head rested on his chest as he held me close.

"Hold your nose. I'm going to submerge you into the water. I want you to relax, keep your nostrils pinched, and be one with the ocean."

When I looked up at him, I saw the swirling stars again. It had a hypnotic effect on me, and I followed his instructions, pinching my nostrils shut, closing my eyes, and tilting my head back. Lono lowered me into the water, his hands supporting my lower back and legs.

Become one with the ocean.

I wasn't sure what that meant? I heard him start to chant in Hawaiian, and although I didn't understand the words, his voice lulled me. Between his soothing voice and the gentle, undulating water, my body went limp. A few minutes later, Lono said, "Okay, experiment over!"

He released me, and my feet touched down on the rocky sand.

"How was that?"

"It was relaxing."

"You were under water for ten minutes."

"*What?*"

He took my right hand and gently placed it over the side of my neck. I wasn't sure what he was doing, but a jolt of shock shot through me as I traced my skin with my fingertips. There were fish-like gills on my neck! I gasped as Lono chuckled at my discomfort.

"What the hell is going on?"

"You didn't know you were part fish?"

I tentatively poked the other side of my neck. "*What is happening?*"

"This is your heritage."

"Holy shit!"

I clamped both my hands along my neck, and the gill-like slits flexed. It was a strange but oddly satisfying feeling. The gills rippled underneath my fingertips, my skin soft and pliable.

"How do I make these go away?"

"Just imagine your neck the way it was before."

I shut my eyes and visualized my neck smooth and flat. When I reached up again, my neck was back to normal, and I sighed with relief.

"Congratulations," Lono said.

"On what?"

"Embracing your true self!"

The day was full of surprises and so much to ponder!

Chapter Eighteen

The days were flying by. Pretty soon, I'd have to go back to California and look for a job, another apartment, and figure out if Rodrigo and I had a future. Despite Lulu's best intentions, adding the clause about keeping me as a tenant would complicate the sale of her house. But for now, I could enjoy hanging out with Diana and Kailani as we sat in the minivan watching rain pelt against the windshield.

We were at Carlsmith Beach, waiting for the rain to clear up so we could swim. Meanwhile, we munched on warm custard malasadas and sipped paper cups of coffee. I'd spent the morning debating with myself on how to share my news with my besties.

I cleared my throat nervously. Diana and Kailani turned toward me with expectant expressions.

"I have something to share with you," I blurted.

"Okay," Diana said.

"I found out I'm part *mano*."

They both had wide-eyed, shocked expressions until Kailani burst out in giggles. "Boy, you really had us going!" she chuckled.

My face flushed with embarrassment. "I'm being serious!" I sputtered.

Diana leaned over and patted my arm. "We still love you… it's all good. People tell me I swim like a dolphin," she added.

"But I can prove it."

I got out of the minivan, the light rain dampening my hair as I edged over to the stone steps and waded into the shallow water.

Diana and Kailani watched as I submerged myself into the cool water. Several minutes went by, and I popped back up, gasping for air. *What the hell?*

"I'm not sure what's happening," I said.

"Maybe you just need more practice?" Kailani said.

"You don't have to prove anything to us," Diana added.

I groaned inwardly. The most transformative thing that ever happened to me, and now I couldn't duplicate it. I did exactly what I'd done before with zero results.

"Maybe you can only do it at the other beach?" Kailani said. "Or… maybe Lono has to be with you?"

I climbed out of the water. Carlsmith Beach was so different than the turtle beach I'd visited with Lono. Here, the rippling, crystalline, aquamarine waves were gentle and sparkling with sunlight. There was even a grassy area to sunbathe. Tall, swaying, coconut palm trees encircled the park and provided limited shade. I noticed several children splashing in a nearby shallow tidepool.

"I like it here. Way calmer and no rocky cliffs to get impaled by," I said.

Diana giggled. "Your mind works in strange ways!"

"You've been to turtle beach," I protested. "Tell me it isn't scary and dangerous."

"You won't get an argument from me," Diana said. "You were crazy to even go there with Lono. I couldn't believe Kailani let you take off like that."

"The ancestors said she would be safe," Kailani interjected.

Kailani was stretched out on her beach towel, her eyes hidden beneath aviator sunglasses. She wore a black tank top underneath short blue denim overalls. I was surprised she took the day off to accompany Diana and me to the beach. In contrast, Diana wore a plum and coral flower print swim dress. Despite the snug wire cups of the bathing suit, her ample breasts spilled out over the top. She sat cross-legged, staring out at the ocean, scanning for any sea turtles while munching on potato chips.

"I thought for sure we'd see some turtles today," Diana said. "I had this feeling they'd show up."

Kailani got a text on her phone and sat up. "It's Cassie," she said. She passed the phone to Diana, who then handed it to me. It was a selfie of Cassie and Steve on Maui on the beach, they were brazenly mugging at the camera. I handed the phone back to Kailani.

"They look happy," Diana said.

Kailani tucked the phone away in her fanny pack nearby.

"I'm glad they worked things out," I said.

"I'm also glad you guys made up," Kailani said. "Cassie felt really bad about what went down between you two."

"She took the first step and apologized. For me, it's in the rear view mirror."

Just a few days ago, I'd received a lavish, orchid, floral arrangement at the lodge. There was a note from Cassie:

"Sorry I lashed out at you. I hope you're still not mad at me. You're a wonderful friend, and I hope we can get past this."

I got up. "I need to use the restroom." I slipped on my sandals and headed toward the public bathrooms, looking back at Kailani and Diana before making a quick detour past the bathrooms.

Whenever Lono was nearby in his turtle form, a strong, briny odor filled my nose, and a warm ticklish sensation fanned down my arms. I hurried over to the lagoon where the children were splashing around, climbed over some craggy rocks, and squatted down and looked over the edge. Beneath a rocky outcropping was a small cave, where I found Lono napping. He was in his turtle form, his leathery head tucked in slightly, his eyes shut.

"Hey," I whispered.

His eyes opened slowly. *You don't have to actually talk to me. You can send me messages telepathically.* The words floated into my mind.

I'm not used to this!

Obviously!

What are you doing here… spying on Kailani and me?

Ha. Don't flatter yourself. I'm visiting with my friend Kaholo. You met him at turtle beach….

The seal! Wow… is he here?

What am I… chopped liver?

I can't get my gills to appear… do I need you to keep helping me? Do I have to be at Turtle Beach?

I felt the ticklish feeling again and wondered if I was sensing his energy, or… if we were energetically bonded because we were both shape shifters?

You have to be patient. You just learned how to do this. The answers to your questions are... both. Get in the water with me and try to flex your gills.

I looked back and saw Kailani and Diana still lounging nearby, then slipped off my cotton beach coverup and kicked off my sandals. I dangled my legs over the rocky precipice.

What're you waiting for? Lono's voice was amused.

I slid over the rocks, scratching my butt in the process. It took me a moment to adjust to the cool water, and I bobbed alongside Lono, feeling the familiar tingling on the sides of my neck and reaching up to touch the delicate slits flexing.

Wow... what did you do?

I didn't do anything. You just believe I have to be around you. Now, just convince yourself you can do it without me. Trying closing the gills.

I brushed my fingertips against the gills and imagined smooth, firm skin. The gills receded.

You see?

I imagined the gills were back and felt the tingling. Dunking under the water, I saw Lono's flippers and back legs floating effortlessly. I closed my eyes and relaxed. It felt great. Now I rustled up my nerve to ask Lono a question I'd been pondering.

What kind of fish am I?

You're a mano.

A shark?

I knew it was my imagination, but Lono appeared to smirk. But turtles didn't have lips.

A shark? I repeated.

What's wrong with being a shark?

Well… I kept imagining myself as a pretty, orange koi.

A goldfish? Why would you want to be a goldfish when you could be a majestic shark? Just wait until you get your fins and tail. Woohoo!

My stomach clenched fearfully.

I'm going to turn into a shark? I don't want that. What if I can't transform back… this is scary!

I started thrashing in the water. I hadn't even considered I could actually transform fully into a shark. My stomach knotted up as I imagined waking up in bed with fins and a tail. The thought terrified me.

Relax. You don't have to fully shapeshift… you get to choose. You can stay with your boring old gills. It'd be fun to terrorize some tourists, though!

Or I could get hunted down like in the Jaws movie. No thanks!

Then… make the most of your shark abilities. They're efficient hunters with great hearing and sense of smell. Isn't that how you knew I was here?

I thought you did that?

Try it now. Hone in the area with your hearing and sense of smell. What do you get?

I closed my eyes and focused. The strong, fragrant scent of plumeria filled my nostrils.

I smell plumeria.

And what does that signify to you?

I shrugged.

Tune it some more. Concentrate. Now what?

Kailani's smiling face floated into my mind. Plumeria was her favorite scent to wear. Just then, I heard my name being called. I looked up to see Kailani and Diana's undulating images above me.

"Noelani!"

Kailani's sharp tone startled me. I bobbed back up the surface to see her and Diana standing over me, stared anxiously. Diana extended her hand to help me out of the water.

"I'm fine," I sputtered.

I was flustered and automatically touched my neck. No gills.

"You were gone for so long, we got worried!" Kailani said.

Diana helped me over the rocks, and I scooted the rest of the way on my butt, awkwardly perching myself on the rocky precipice.

"Sorry, I lost track of time. I was talking to Lono and got caught up in our conversation."

Diana looked perplexed. *"Lono?* Is he here?"

I glanced over at Kailani, who smiled with understanding.

"He swims here almost every day. He meets up with his friend Kaholo. Isn't that right, Kailani?" I said.

"That's right!" Kailani affirmed. Her eyes sparkled and I could tell she was trying not to laugh.

"They just left."

Diana looked at Kailani and then at me. "You girls are acting funny!"

"It's an inside joke about Lono," Kailani said. "It's a long story."

"I thought I saw a turtle over here, so we came over. Thank God we did, because we found you floating around." Diana said.

"Sorry I worried you both," I said.

"Let's get something to eat," Diana said.

As we walked toward Kailani's minivan, my phone buzzed. *It's Rodrigo!*

"Hey!" I said with excitement.

"Finally… we're actually talking live," he said. "It's only been two weeks since I heard your voice."

"Really?"

"I know… time flies when you're having fun," he replied dryly.

We'd been playing telephone tag since I landed on the island. With the three-hour time difference and lack of cell phone coverage at the lodge, it was hard to connect in real time. Mostly we'd traded awkward voice mails and texts.

"I've missed you, babe," Rodrigo added.

I hesitated. I did miss him, but I hadn't even noticed two weeks had already passed.

"I'm glad we're finally connecting," I said finally. "I miss hearing your voice."

"You're still coming back next week, right?"

Kailani and Diana had walked ahead of me to give me privacy. I watched as they opened the minivan doors to air out the humid car.

"I think so."

"What does *that* mean?"

"Kailani offered me a job!"

"*Okay.*"

I felt the apprehension in his voice.

"I'm still mulling it over."

"I heard your ex-husband turned up."

"Who told you that?"

"Cassie texted me. She was worried about you."

"He did but it was nothing. I'm sorry she bothered you."

"It's no bother. Maybe I should come out—I'm overdue for some time off."

"No… I mean if you want to… but I'm fine and I'll be back soon."

"Are you sure… I've got plenty of vacation time saved up."

I wonder what else Cassie told him?

"I'm with Kailani and Diana… could we chat tonight? I can call you from the lodge kitchen on the landline."

"Okay. I love you, babe."

"Okay."

I hung up feeling foolish. I hadn't expected him to say that. I caught up with Kailani and Diana, and they looked at me expectantly.

"I can't believe Cassie texted Rodrigo to call me. *Ugh.*"

"I'm sure she meant well," Kailani said.

"He said he loves me," I blurted.

"*And?*" Diana asked.

"I was so shocked, I just hung up."

"A lot of women would love to have your problem," Diana said. "A sexy, handsome, younger man who's crazy about you!"

"*Look!*"

We all turned and looked up to find a shimmering, brilliant rainbow forming a perfect arc over the ocean. The bands of blue, green, yellow, pink and red contrasted starkly against the milky white clouds and cerulean sky.

"I never get tired of this!" Diana breathed.

"Look, it's a *double* rainbow!" Kailani said.

We looked up to see a fainter arc over the brighter rainbow.

"We are blessed," Diana said reverently.

We savored the moment, feeling the warm sun on our faces, the briny air and the joy of witnessing nature's miracle. Then we reluctantly got into the minivan, Kailani started the engine, and looked up at the rearview mirror at me with a smile. "You'll figure it out," she said.

I sat in the backseat as she backed up and navigated our way toward the open road. Glancing back at the beach, the rainbow had faded.

***

The coqui frogs were going full blast outside the kitchen. I sat perched on a high stool facing the long, wooden dining table that served as the buffet bar. The sultry day left a lingering heat in the room along with the delicious scent of lemongrass and ginger.

Kailani had outdone herself with a tasty tofu stir fry for our dinner. The wooden ceiling fan churned lazily above me and provided a modest breeze as I took in the peacefulness of the empty room. *I could get used to this.*

Kailani and Diana had retired to their respective abodes, and I enjoyed the solitude. I hadn't realized how stressed I was with the divorce proceedings. I'd splurged on a massage or two and kept my appointments with my therapist, but all the tension had shown up in my tight shoulders and a sense of ongoing foreboding. I'd overcompensated by chugging down more coffee. Now, I was sleeping better and woke up refreshed. I went on walks and drank green tea in the morning.

I was antsy about calling Rodrigo, still wondering about what to say to him. I did care about him, but I wasn't sure if I was in love with him. I was looking forward to going home and being with him. Then there was the thorny topic about how much to disclose? I was still processing my newly discovered identity as part *mano*, let alone disclosing that my new bestie was a turtle.

But somehow, I knew Rodrigo would understand, and my fretting was just an old trigger from the past. I'd tried hard to be the perfect partner to Jason but for some reason didn't insist he be a good partner to me. I clung to the naïve notion that being in a partnership meant telling each other everything— that full transparency was the magic bullet to a long and thriving marriage. Yet that hadn't worked out for me. I could drive myself crazy speculating why it wasn't obvious he'd been unfaithful to me, but what good would *that* do? Despite being together twenty years, he'd rarely expressed his feelings for me. He said *I love you* when I said it first, but I had consoled myself with how prodigious our lovemaking was. Up until the end, it had been enough he found me sexually attractive. Still, everything revolved around his image of being successful with an attractive wife as an accessory. I'd played into that with no questions asked.

At the end of the day, he hadn't chosen to fight for us. What I wanted didn't matter.

The phone rang suddenly, startling me.

"Hello?"

"Hi, babe!"

"I didn't know you had the lodge phone number!"

"It's on the website. I thought you were going to call me like ten minutes ago? Are you okay?"

"Sorry about that. I seem to lose track of time around here."

"You sound good."

"*I do?*"

"Yeah… more relaxed. Sounds like you're enjoying spending time with your peeps."

"I was thinking you should save your vacation time. You could use them to see your family or something."

Rodrigo fell silent. My heart was pounding uncomfortably. *I'm making a mess of things.* I wanted to reassure him I was okay… that he didn't need to race here to rescue me from my ex-husband.

"I know you don't feel the same about me. I know it's too soon to ask for a commitment, but you're part of my life now. I couldn't imagine us *not* being together," Rodrigo blurted.

I was touched by his vulnerable outburst. *Would Jason ever say something that sensitive and revealing?*

"Kailani offered me a job. She wants me to move here and help out at the lodge."

"Is that what you want?"

"I'm not sure. It would be a fresh start."

"So, where would that leave *us*?"

"All I can say is that I want to be with you, too. I don't know what that looks like yet."

"I'm glad you're talking about us in the future tense. *I love you!*"

"I love you too, and I can't wait to see you."

We hung up, and I realized this time that it seemed natural to say it.

Chapter Nineteen

Kailani and I were eating breakfast at Hawaiian Style Café in Hilo. I watched her wolf down a big plate of banana macnut pancakes as I lingered over my coffee and omelet. How did such a small person eat so much and not gain weight, especially since we were both post-menopausal? I felt like looking at my hashbrowns put five pounds on my butt already!

"Thanks for breakfast, *sista*," Kailani said.

"It's the least I can do for letting me stay at the lodge,"

"We're *family*."

A pleasant warm, fuzzy feeling filled my chest at her words.

"Do you think Jason is still here? Have the ancestors spoken?"

"What do *you* perceive? You can commune with the ancestors too."

I shook my head and shrugged.

"It's simple. You just tell them you'd like their guidance, and they'll jump in. Believe me, I wish I could shut them off. They love to chat with me! It's been that way since we were kids… you know that."

I guess I always knew Kailani was special and had uncanny prescience. It was just a part of her that I'd gotten used to and didn't question.

"I remember the time we were on that school field trip to the aquarium, and you screamed for the van driver to stop."

She nodded. "That was a crazy day."

"If you hadn't yelled, the van would have run over that guy on the motorcycle!"

I recalled that day vividly. We had been eleven years old and headed for a fun day at the aquarium during a misty day in San Francisco. At a busy intersection, there was a motorcycle in front of us. When the light changed, Kailani yelled, "STOP!" The man on the motorcycle had raced to get across the intersection on the slick, damp street and flipped the bike over.

"Remember how the rider flew off and nearly landed on the hood of the van? Thanks to you, the man survived with minor scrapes!"

"Remember our van driver, Mr. Weisman? He got out and starting chain smoking cigarettes!" Kailani said with a laugh.

"What crazy childhoods we had."

Then a thought popped into my head. "Are you part shark too?"

"No, I'm not. I'm something else."

"Are you going to tell me?

She smiled. "What do you think I am?"

"I don't know… you're not going to tell me? We always told each other everything."

"I'll leave it to you to figure out. It's pretty obvious."

"Not to me."

"So… what's going on with you and Rodrigo?"

"Well, I said the 'L' word to him last night."

"And…?"

"It felt good. I do love him, but I'm not sure what that means in the big picture."

"You're overthinking it."

"*Probably*. Jason said that was one of my biggest flaws. I have a hard time being in the moment, I was always fearful of the future."

"Like he didn't have character flaws. Forget Jason… focus on Rodrigo… he's your future."

Kailani's prognostications were always accurate. Why doubt her now?

***

Diana met Kailani and me at the Stack and Save in Hilo to stock up on groceries. The next guests would be arriving in a few days, and we were stocking up on basics. I trailed Diana and Kailani absently as they loaded up the grocery cart, knowing there was something I had left to do—I couldn't move on with Rodrigo until I settled things with Jason.

I dreaded confrontations, but I needed closure. Maybe I could call him or write him a letter… or send an email. None of the options were palatable. Finally, I decided to call upon the ancestors. *Look, guys… help me out here. I need closure!*

I waited for a sign, but nothing happened, so I followed my two girlfriends as they headed out to the parking lot. They began to load up the minivan with bags of groceries, and a young man from the grocery store came over to retrieve the shopping carts. He turned toward me with a sweet smile.

"Are you having a good day, Miss?""

"I am… thanks."

"You have something important to do today, don't you?"

I looked over at Kailani and Diana, who were leaning against the minivan, staring curiously at me.

"I do?"

"My *tutu* always tells me to give messages when I hear her voice. She is telling me you have someone to meet. She said the words *free yourself!"*

Before I could react, he cheerfully gathered the shopping carts and began pushing them back to the store.

"What was that all about?" Diana asked.

"I'm not sure," I said.

I got into the passenger side of the minivan with a strong feeling we needed to go to the Hilo airport.

"We need to go to the airport!" I blurted.

Kailani was startled. "Okay. Let's do it."

She started the engine and backed the car out of the parking lot. I looked up at Diana through the rearview mirror.

The ancestors have led me faithfully up to this point, so now I have to trust.

"I'm not going crazy, I promise."

She threw her hands up in mock surrender. "Never doubted it."

My stomach clenched up nervously, and I wondered if I *was* going crazy. Something told me Jason was there.

The airport wasn't too far away, and as we got close, I had another insight.

"Wait… sorry. Could you please pull over by the rental car agency? By the green awning."

When we pulled up, we saw Jason standing on the sidewalk with a rental car representative. He was dressed in his Elvis shirt over khaki cargo shorts and beige flip flops. I could tell he was upset by his flushed face. They were looking at a white SUV with a severely dented front fender. I got out slowly and heard them arguing.

"I am not responsible for this," Jason seethed. "A crow landed on the windshield and started flapping its wings and distracted me!"

The car agency representative shrugged and began snapping photos with his cell phone. "I'm sorry to hear that, sir, but I need to document this. It might fall under our *acts of God* policy and may not be covered."

"*What the hell?* Acts of God… are you shitting me?"

"Jason," I called.

He looked up, and his eyes widened in shock. "Could my day get any *worse?*" he moaned. He took a step toward me. "What're you doing here?" he demanded.

"Looks like you had a bit of a fender bender."

"You think?" he groused. "It's been a total shit show since I got here. My flight was delayed *twice,* my hotel reservation was cancelled, and now *this!*"

He flung his arms up in frustration. Something about the dire situation made me giggle, which infuriated him.

"What are you doing here?"

"I forgive you for lying about Candace."

"You *forgive* me?" he echoed. His mouth formed a hard line, and his voice was cold. "I turned to Candace because she was the only one who cared about me losing the restaurant. It certainly wasn't you. You didn't give a *shit* that the restaurant meant everything to me. I put all my blood, sweat, and tears into it, and all you did was whine about the money!"

Kailani gently put her hand on my back, trying to be supportive.

"And you didn't care about how that damn restaurant sucked the life out of our marriage. It always meant more to you than me!" I yelled back.

Jason rolled his eyes at me. In that moment, everything came into sharp focus. *Why didn't I realize what a petty and self-absorbed asshole he was?* Jason put his hand up as if banishing me.

"I don't have time for this. Go off with your *boy toy* and live your life. I frankly don't give a flying fuck."

"Your obsession with the restaurant ruined our marriage. All you cared about was being successful and getting five-star reviews… and getting drunk!"

"Oh my God, are you being serious? You enjoyed the perks that came with that. Candace was my lifeline when *you* gave up on us."

"*You* gave up on us. I gave you money to keep the restaurant afloat. You lied to me about Candace, and your drinking killed our marriage."

It was falling on deaf ears. He turned away from me and waved me off. His dismissive gesture infuriated me.

"I don't need this *shit*. Have a nice life," he muttered.

"*Go fuck yourself*," I yelled.

Kailani grabbed my wrist and pulled me away.

"Let's get out of here. Don't waste any more energy on that *shit heel!*"

She half dragged, half shoved me back into the minivan. Diana was whooping it up loudly and applauding.

"Man, I wished I got that on my phone. You were great!" Diana said.

Kailani started up the engine and peeled the minivan away from the curb. "I'm proud of you, girlfriend. You really stood up for yourself!"

There was something about her in that moment. Her dark, all-knowing eyes—and I realized… she was a *crow!*

Chapter Twenty

It was peaceful to float on the waves. The salty ocean water lapped over my body as my gills flexed in rhythm to the gently undulating water. The uncertainty and anxiety that had plagued me for months evaporated as I allowed myself the pleasure of embodying my *mano* self.

Patterns of dappled light formed behind my closed eyes, and I took in a deep breath as a vision of Jason flashed in. I saw him walking away from Candace, his face an unhappy grimace. I saw Candace's tear-stained face as she watched him leave. Sorrow rippled through me as I sensed her pain.

Lono's voice popped into my mind *"Let go. Let the ocean water cleanse your spirit and release any attachment to him. Your future lies with someone else."*

Tears began to stream down my face, mingling with the briny seawater. Candace's sorrow had triggered my own that I'd suppressed. I let the tears flow freely, and with each gentle wave, released the past… released Jason.

In the distance, I heard Kailani calling to me. I turned my head and saw her on the beach, waving both arms at me. I reluctantly flipped over on my belly and swam leisurely back to shore. As I emerged onto the sand, Kailani shook her head at me with a smile. We were at Pine Trees beach near the Kona airport. The pearly-platinum coarse sand was warm between my toes as the limpid azure-blue water rippled in placid waves over the rocky tidepools. Fluffy, ivory, cumulus clouds hung low in the turquoise blue sky. Except for a few beachcombing tourists, we had the area to ourselves.

"You've been under for almost two hours!"

"*Really?*"

Time drifted away when I was doing my *mano* practice. She handed me a beach towel to dry myself off.

"So, you're not going to go full-on *mano*?"

I shook my head firmly. "Nope."

I was still learning, and the fear that I might be stuck in my shark body still unnerved me. I was content with having gills and being able swim effortlessly through the waves. After I toweled myself off, I sank down on the sand beside Kailani. She handed me a bamboo fork and a container of cut up fruit with a honey yogurt dressing.

"You need to eat."

I dug into the chunks of mango, papaya, and banana enthusiastically.

"You going to tell Rodrigo about your gills?" Kailani asked with an impish smile.

"*No way,*" I replied. "Maybe someday, but I'm still figuring this out!"

"Probably a good idea. I didn't tell Shara for like a year."

"How'd she take it?"

Kailani sighed. "She already knew. She suspected it but waited for me to tell her. I was a nervous wreck."

"Why?"

She shrugged. "Fear of being rejected. Lingering childhood baggage about being accepted."

"I'm not sure how Rodrigo would react. He's pretty accepting of most things in general. He was a little perturbed about Lono—thought that we were hooking up."

"You're kidding. You didn't tell him Lono was gay?"

It was my turn to shrug. "I don't feel it was my place to out people… not that Lono would care."

A crow flew over us, and I shaded my eyes and watched as it winged over the ocean. "One of your friends?" I asked.

Kailani laughed. "We're not all related."

"Was that you on my skylight back in California?" I asked. Kailani cocked her head to one side with an amused smile. She reminded me of the crow in the mango tree at Turtle Beach. *Well… except it really was her!* Why hadn't I figured this out before… her jet black hair, her dark brown, almost black eyes that astutely surveyed everything around her. Her dainty feet with toes that curled down slightly. Her love of peanuts and berries.

"No, that wasn't me. I can fly only so far!" she joked. "It was probably one of my relatives looking out for you."

I shook my head as if to clear the cobwebs in my brain. I was still processing all the incredible epiphanies from the past two weeks. My bestie Kailani being a crow, Lono a turtle, and me… *a shark!*

"Is Diana an animal too?"

Kailani shook her head. "Only those of us that have native blood."

"When did you first know about your crow self?"

Kailani thoughtfully scooped up a handful of sand and let it sift through her fingers.

"Tutu knew before I did. She'd watch me and mentored me, since she was a *Nene goose*. The first time I actually flew—it was the most amazing feeling. I think I was five!" Kailani's face glowed at the memory.

I wished I'd had that kind of maternal nurturing and support. Instead, I'd been burdened with an anxious and narrow-minded caretaker. I pushed away the jab of envy that bubbled up inside me and reached over to grab the canteen we'd brought, sipping some water.

"If Aunt Lily had seen my gills, she would have gotten a Catholic priest to perform an exorcism!"

Kailani chuckled. "She wasn't that bad!"

"She *was*… trust me."

"I know she loved you, she tried her best. She knew you were different, and I think it worried her. Tutu tried to talk to her about your uniqueness, but your aunt shut her down. I'm sorry that she was so hard on you."

I sighed. "It's all right. She sent me a nice note after we sent out the wedding invitations."

Aunt Lily had sent back the custom-designed, vintage RSVP card with a handwritten note on the back. *"To my lovely niece. You deserve all the happiness in the world. So glad you found someone who will always love and care for you."*

"I remember that. Didn't you have it framed as a keepsake?"

I nodded. "She wasn't a sentimental person, so that note meant a lot."

The memory of opening the card and reading her message brought a smile to my face. At the end, Aunt Lily had tried to reach out in her own way.

"Sista!"

I looked up to see Lono striding toward us with a handsome male friend. He was carrying snorkeling gear—a glass mask, plastic snorkel, and rubber flippers. He dropped his gear on the sand as Kailani and I got up. We shared a warm group hug. His friend seemed vaguely familiar to me. He was slightly taller than Lono, with thick, dark, shoulder-length, wavy hair. He had a similar build as Lono's with a slender, toned body. His friend leaned over and hugged me.

"So nice to see you again, *Sista*," he said.

I pulled back in confusion. "I don't think we've met,"

Lono grinned, "Sure you have. This is *Kahalo*."

Kahalo... the priestess seal.

"I had no idea," I sputtered.

"*Obviously*," Kailani teased.

Lono nodded, "Isn't your man arriving for some R and R today?"

My man. Rodrigo. A pleasant warmth fanned through me.

"Then they're flying back to California," Kailani added. "Hopefully to pack up and move here."

Lono put a hand on my shoulder and squeezed, "Enjoy yourself, Noelani. That's what life is all about... celebrating the moment."

"We'd love to see you two at the lodge, but you both have a lot of catching up!" Kailani said with a wink.

Lono, Kailani, and Kahalo laughed, and Lono put his arm around my shoulders. "See you soon."

I watched the two walk away, holding hands.

"So, they're *together*?"

Kailani smiled. *"Obviously."* She playfully punched my arm, and we plopped back down on the beach towel. Rodrigo's plane would be landing soon. My stomach fluttered with nervous energy.

Kailani leaned over and patted my back. "It'll be fine. You've got a good man in Rodrigo."

"Well, I thought Jason was a good man, too," I fretted.

She shrugged, "He *was* in the beginning. But he wanted a trophy wife more than an actual partner. He fell in love with your looks… not your soul."

Ouch.

"I didn't think he was that shallow… *was he?*"

Kailani raised her eyebrows. "He was always showering you with expensive jewelry and clothes. He always wanted to show you off at the restaurant to meet investors… *hello?*"

"I sold all that jewelry. I was surprised how detached I was when I hauled it all to the consignment store."

"You were ready to let Jason go. I think you finally realized it had all been a façade. You're so brave!"

"*You* helped me through this. You and Lono helped me reconnect to the ancestors and discover my inner mano!" I joked.

"Shark energy is powerful. They are the apex predator of the oceans!"

We bumped fists over that.

"Forget about sprouting fins and a tail. Immersing yourself in the full mano beingness means tapping into that innate sense of direction and being adaptable. This is *all you.* You've come so far, *Sista!*"

I *had* come far, and I was ready to embrace my future with courage that everything would fall into place—I didn't have to plan anything. Just let life unfold.

* * *

We didn't leave our condo rental for three days. Between Door Dash take-out meals and some groceries we'd picked up, we hunkered down and stayed inside.

"You should go away more often," Rodrigo teased. "It turns you into a sex maniac!"

"Look who's talking."

We lounged on top of the king-sized bed, the ceiling fan whirling above us. The only other sound was the noisy rattling of the window AC unit.

"We should go out. You've never been to Kona, and there's so much to see," I said.

"I like my view just fine."

He cupped my breast for emphasis, and I swatted his hand away playfully.

"*Seriously*. We should go out tonight… check out the area."

"I've been to Hawaii before, I'm good." Rodrigo leaned back against the pillows. "I'll take you out for dinner if you want. Otherwise, I'm happy to relax and stare endlessly at your naked self."

I reflected on our first day together. How seeing him walking toward me at the Kona airport made me so giddy and nervous at the same time. Yet his tender hug had been familiar and comforting. Then we'd driven to Don's Mai Tai Bar for lunch at their open air restaurant. We'd wolfed down coconut shrimp and tuna poke bowls and sat at the bar overlooking the sparkling Pacific Ocean. We saw silver flashes of leaping dolphins in the distance and migrating whales as they spouted flumes of water into the air through their blowholes. Then, after a brief tropical downpour, a vertical rainbow magically materialized. Brilliant bands of blue, yellow, orange, and red appeared and then vanished.

"I can't believe two days just evaporated. Only three days left, and we go home."

"We can stay longer. I'll just call in sick. I'll be exhausted after five days of non-stop sex, so it'll be the truth."

"I don't want you to get into trouble."

"Too late for that."

I got up to get a sip of water. I definitely needed to keep hydrated. Rodrigo's eyes followed me as I went into the kitchen and grabbed a bottle of cold water from the 'fridge.

"You make up your mind about Kailani's job offer?" he asked. He was propped up on one elbow, laying on his side, studying me.

I opened the bottled water and sipped. "I'm still thinking about it. It'd be a big move… I'd have to put everything in storage and ship my car over. And… there's *you*."

"*Moi?*" Rodrigo fluttered his eyes comically.

"Would you… move with me?"

"You mean, like… shack up?"

"Kailani offered me a cabin to live in. I'm sure it'd fit two people… if you were interested."

"Hell yes—I'm all in. "

"Don't you want to think about it?"

He shook his head. "What's to think about… sun, surf, and my lady running around naked. Yeah, baby!"

He patted the empty spot next to him on the bed. "Just go easy on me."

"I think you have that backward!" I climbed back in bed.

He leaned over and tenderly brushed some stray hair off my face. "No, I got it right."

He leaned over and lightly kissed me. Then we curled up together, spoon-style. I would be moving again in less than a year, my life turned upside down once more. I sighed.

"What is it, babe? You okay?"

"Just thinking about the transition to here," I said. "Lots of moving parts."

He smiled and his face radiated pure love for me. "It'll be easy breezy… we'll be together. That's all that matters."

The future didn't frighten me anymore. There would be more adventures and stories ahead. I would grow more into my *mano* self and hang out with Lono, Kahalo, and Kailani in both their animal and human forms.

Lono's recent words popped into my head: "Enjoy yourself, Noelani. That's what life is all about… celebrating the moment."

Rodrigo draped his arm over my waist, and as he gently dozed off, a bubble of contentment enveloped me—I was *home*.

AVAILABLE NOW:
The Honu Diary
Book 2 of the Pono Trilogy
@nicolasluv

www.ingramcontent.com/pod-product-compliance
Lightning Source LLC
Chambersburg PA
CBHW060448300726
48975CB00008B/2438